Sweet

Escape

Lexie Syrah

Sweet Escape

Copyright

All Characters in this Book are over the age of 18.

This book contains strong sexual content

Prologue

Do not weep for the ones that died, for their pain is over. Save your tears for the ones that live, for the ones that still have torment to bear.

Aurora's eyes stared lifelessly at her daughter. She'd been a good mother, a loving mother. Now she was gone. All that was left was a shell and a slowly moving river of blood that threatened to connect her to the daughter that she'd left.

If she'd known what her daughter's life would be like, she would have strangled the child in her bed. If those lifeless eyes had seen the things that would happen to her daughter, she would have killed both of them.

The world is a cruel place, but the men who stood over Aurora's lifeless body were crueler than the rest. They stared down at her daughter, Maia. She was in shock. Shaking and silent, she stared into her mother's cold, dead eyes.

The men looked at the eleven-year-old with smiles on their faces. Another whore for the cages.

The young ones were more valuable. Not young enough that they had to worry about permanent damage when their customers were done for the night, but young enough that the pedos would still get hard.

The girl just stared at her dead mother. They all did this. She'd wake up eventually. Especially once she had a cock in her. Stretching and tearing, she'd wake up screaming.

The girl didn't know that of course. She just thought that her life was over. It wasn't though. No, it would have been better for her if it had, but her life would continue on for many years, and she would scream in pain for the rest of them.

The river of red kept running towards Maia. Oozing and creeping, the last bit of Aurora's life yearned to touch her, to stain her, to help the girl to remember that there had been a person who loved her. The men took her by the arm before it could touch her, before it could leave even a temporary reminder of the woman who had loved her more than anything.

Now there was no one. Nothing. No feeling except pain. No sound except screaming. No one except monsters.

Chapter 1: Pain

*The pain of torment is temporary, but
the scars are forever.*

I fell into my cell without a sound. I felt the skin of my knee rip as my body hit the concrete floor, but I barely noticed it. This new pain didn't compare to the pain that coursed through my back from the purple spots already beginning to appear.

I'd been so happy when I'd felt the man's cock enter my ass. It had meant that the beating was going to end. The pain of him being inside me was nothing compared to the pain from those terrible wooden dowels that he'd used on my back. He'd built a rhythm to his beating, as though there had been a drumming in his head that he was trying to bring it into the world using my body as a human instrument.

Pain had been a constant for as long as I could remember. Ever since the day I'd been taken. My holes always hurt. All of them. Every day. That's what happened when you were owned and used as a whore. I had been used by someone at least once per day for the last eight years.

I crawled across the dirty cell to the table. Sometimes my legs didn't like to work very well after I'd been tied down for too long. The tingling angered me. I had to stay awake for the pain, why didn't my legs have to? Why did they get a reprieve from the pain?

I pulled myself into the wooden chair as my legs woke up. The table beside it held medical supplies, any that I could have found a use for. I'd been taught from an early age how to bandage my own wounds, how to soothe the aches and pains of my body. It wasn't for my own comfort. No, nothing was for my comfort.

A slave who had infections or uncared for wounds was not a slave that would earn very much money. No one wanted to fuck a woman with oozing sores. I'd refused at first, hoping that the infection would kill me. That had been a mistake. Instead of letting me die from the infections, they'd given me to a true torturer.

I had been tied to a bed, and a doctor had cleaned my wounds, cutting out the infected tissue. He hadn't given me anything for the pain. I'd screamed and fought, but the knife took bit after bit of flesh from the infected section of my back. He was slow about it, enjoying every bit of pain he forced into my body.

I had always taken care of myself after that. They wouldn't let me die, not from something as slow as infection. I was too valuable. No, they would make sure that I stayed alive.

I rubbed the antiseptic salve across my knee and put a bandage on it to protect it while the blood clotted. Then I rubbed a different salve over my bruises. It would help to prevent serious bruising. Everyone wanted a fresh canvas to paint with torment.

The tingling in my legs was almost gone, and I hobbled to the bed. A bowl of mush sat on a tray. Mush was the only kind of food that I was allowed. I could try to wedge larger food into my throat and choke myself to death. They wouldn't allow that, so all I got was mush.

This was vegetable and meat mush. One of my favorites. It was like someone had chewed up a stew and spit it into the bowl. It didn't look good, but it kept me healthy and was filling enough to keep my body going when I had new wounds every day.

Life had become a simple set of repetitions. Eight years of repetition. Eight years of pain. Eight years of being a sex slave.

I knew what came next, and I didn't shy away from it.

I swallowed the mush down. They would know if I tried to starve myself. Then I got down on my knees and put my arms behind my back, hands gripping the opposite elbows. I already heard the clicking of hard boot soles as they walked down the concrete hallway to my cell. I looked down at the ground in front of me, not looking upward at the man who would be enjoying my body next.

The door to my cell opened, and Marcos stepped through. Jet black hair, greasy and cut short. Dark brown eyes that looked down at me. Tan skin of a Mexican. Everyone was Mexican here. All of the men that used my body at least.

I stared at the ground as he stood in front of me, my eyes focused on the black leather boots that he wore. The same boots that everyone in the complex wore. Tall boots that climbed all the way up to the middle of the calf. On the side was emblazoned a shiny silver star. It was a part of the uniform that all of the guards wore. Marcos didn't wear a guard's uniform, but he still wore those boots that I saw every day.

"That beating looked like it hurt, Maia, but you still managed to cum when he fucked your ass, didn't you?"

"Yes sir." I always came for the men that used me. Even when I didn't want to.

"Are you going to cum for me when I fuck you today?" he asked, but he already knew the answer.

"Yes sir." That was the only one answer he ever wanted.

His pants hit the ground in front of me, and he ran his hands through my hair. "Looks like it's time for a shower. Maybe tomorrow. How does that sound?"

"Yes sir."

"I'll enjoy hearing you scream while they wax you," he said. His cock hit the side of my face and I opened my mouth. He didn't need to say anything.

He slowly pushed his cock to the back of my throat nonchalantly as he continued, "Today was your birthday, did you know that?"

I used to gag when men used my throat, but not anymore. Now their cocks just slipped down my throat without any resistance. My body had become a perfect vessel for them to use, molded and shaped for the one task of pleasing men in any way that they desire.

"And for your birthday, I've gotten you a very special gift. A man has bought you for an entire day, not just for a few hours like the rest. He told me that he wanted a woman that he wouldn't have to force. He wants a woman who will hurt herself for him, a woman who knows how to keep going even when she's screaming."

His cock filled my throat and I tried to let his words slide past me without taking hold, but the fear that filled me was a tangible thing. A man was going to force me to hurt myself all day. Pain and torment were normal, but it was usually only for a few hours per day.

Marcos enjoyed doing this, talking to me as he fucked my mouth. He didn't want a conversation. He wanted to feel my fear and my pain while he filled my throat. It wasn't the worst I'd experienced. At least he was slow about it.

He pulled out of my throat and slowly stroked himself in front of me. "I'm going to have him video tape the entire thing so that we can watch it together. You'll enjoy that, won't you, Maia?"

"Yes sir," I said softly.

"I knew you would," he said as he walked to my bed and sat on the edge of it. I followed him, my eyes still looking down at the ground. I straddled his legs and lowered myself to let his cock fill my pussy.

"Maia, why would you want my cock in your pussy? If you're going to cum, it has to hurt, remember?"

I didn't want to cum. I'd already cum today. What I wanted was a knife to cut Marcos's throat, to watch the blood drain and pool on the floor, but I would have settled for a nap.

I raised myself up, letting his cock slip out of me. I noted how wet I already was. My body knew how to minimize the pain.

"Wait Maia, your pussy dripped all over my cock. Why don't you suck all your juices off. I know how badly you want to cum, so I want to make sure it hurts enough." Of course it would hurt. He knew that. It didn't matter if he was lubed up or not since the man from earlier had raped my ass for damn near an hour.

That didn't matter though. Marcos was here to enjoy hurting me. He had trained me for it. He'd forced my body to reject all sexual pleasure if it didn't have pain associated with it, and I hated him for it. Now, instead of enjoying an orgasm, I knew that it was just one more trick I was doing for him and his customers.

But I was a slave, and Marcos wasn't doing this for me. I climbed off him and got onto my knees in front of him. I took his cock into my mouth and cleaned him. I didn't hesitate as most people would. This wasn't anything for me. Just another task.

I tried to leave plenty of saliva on his cock. Marcos would know that I was doing that. He'd give me that much. Just a little bit of spit wouldn't stop it from hurting, wouldn't stop him from drawing the pain from my body.

I stood up and faced away from him, straddling his cock before I sat down on him. My asshole swallowed his cock easily enough. I was no stranger to it. His hands went to my waist, but he didn't push me down or try to control me. Other men did. They liked to hurt me with their own hands.

Marcos wanted me to do it to myself. He knew that the spit would dry up in seconds and then it would be like someone was rubbing sandpaper across my insides. Burning and scratching me. I would keep going though.

His hands ran up and down my waist before they went to my breasts. He always talked about how pretty my tits were, how he loved how they bounced when I rode him. His fingers closed around my nipples and pulled down.

Sharp pain ran through my breasts and I grit my teeth, but I felt my pussy begin to pulse with need. My body wanted the pain. It wanted to cum again. Every bit of me hated the way that he had trained my body to do this, but I couldn't stop the way that it reacted now.

And I let out a moan. Low and loud, my voice filled the room. You wouldn't be able to tell that I was furious. A split happened every time a man brought pain to my body. My body worked to find sexual release, and my mind watched. Furious and filled with rage.

Up and down, I bounced on his cock, and the burning began to fill me. My nipples felt like they were being torn. I didn't look at any of it. My eyes were focused on the opposite side of the room.

"You're such a good little painslut, Maia. Why aren't more girls built like you? Built to be broken, day after day. If only I could make your whore holes virgin every morning so that I could rip you again. That would be the only way that I could make you any better of a whore."

His words fell on deaf ears as my breath quickened. In and out. In and out. Pain was everywhere now. If he left my body alone and just let me hurt, I would cum soon.

His fingers released my nipples though, and I groaned. I needed that pain. A burning asshole just wasn't enough anymore. Marcos's hands found my waist again, and he gripped me. Not to force my body anywhere. No, he kept letting me bring the pain on myself.

Instead, his thumbs found the deep purple bruises that had come to the surface of my skin. He pressed deeply into the bruises and I screamed. He hadn't been this cruel in a long time. I tried to get away, but this time, he held me.

He held me, and he dug his thumbs into my bruises. Aching spots that covered my back where wooden dowels had bruised me deep down below the skin.

His cock throbbed in my ass as I screamed even louder. I felt the orgasm rip through me. Angry and fearsome, it gave life to my broken body. I escaped his grasp even as he came, squirting his cum all over his legs instead of into my ass.

A wicked grin curled across his face as he stood up, his cum dripping from his legs to the floor. "It

They weren't just sexual about it, and they spent a long time spraying her face as she sputtered trying to catch her breath. There was no reason for them to act like this. They just enjoyed making her miserable.

And I watched from one of the two-sided windows that filled the entire prison complex. Concrete floors and concrete columns were the structures that supported the massive building, but instead of walls, two-sided glass was everywhere that I'd been allowed. This way, anyone walking the halls could see who was being tortured in each room, but they could do it in relative anonymity.

That was how I watched Maia. This was not my world. A business associate had told me that they knew a place where I could find whores who were better than any others, and they weren't expensive. I'd found my way here, and I was overwhelmed by the activities that some of them participated in.

They were preparing her for me. I'd bought her for the day. That's how long it would take me to do what I needed to do.

I watched as one of the men took a syringe from the table and pressed the needle against her ass and pushed it in slowly. She didn't squirm or try to get away from the needle. It must have been the depo shot that all of the slaves were put on. One shot every three months and no pregnant women or unwanted babies to deal with.

The man walked away from her, and I couldn't help but stare at her. She was beautiful. I didn't know how anyone had broken her to this point. It was almost painful knowing just how innocent she had to have been when she'd been brought here. The people here were monsters to be able to break a girl that young, to hurt her so thoroughly that she was compliant to anything like these girls were.

I couldn't turn away as they stopped cleaning her and began waxing her. Strip after strip of wax was ripped off her freshly scoured body. Already, her skin had been made sensitive. Thin strips bled where the skin had been scrubbed too harshly or where the wax had been pulled poorly.

This must have been hell for her. Marcos had told me that she'd been here for eight years. She'd been subjected to this torment from the very beginning.

Rape and torture had been the only things she'd known since then. How would she ever recover and become a normal human being? How would anyone ever help her become anything more than afraid? Maybe killing her would be a mercy compared to what I planned.

I shivered as they finished waxing her. Instead of rubbing an aloe vera gel over her body like most places would, they poured rubbing alcohol over her body.

She'd stayed silent the entire time, but the alcohol must have burned like fire because she screamed and shook in the ropes that suspended her and bound her. Her back arched, and her muscles clenched, and instead of feeling sympathetic, the men that were preparing her simply laughed.

Monsters. This entire place was filled with monsters. Maybe Maia would never be able to recover from this place. Maybe she would beg me to kill her. I would do it for her. After seeing this place, I knew that if she begged me, I would kill her and be happy that she finally found peace.

For now, I needed to prepare myself for the day. My plans were not as simple as most of her customers were, and there were still things that needed to be taken care of.

Chapter 3: Fear

The woman didn't fear death. How could one who knew only pain be afraid of the end of it?

I woke up in a room outside of the compound. A room that I'd never seen before. I tried to get up and realized that I wore a dress made of soft cotton. My arms and legs were bound to a chair. My mind felt fuzzy, and I realized that I'd been drugged.

I must have been drugged by whoever was buying me. That was the only reason that I wouldn't remember exactly what had happened. I knew that I was led out of my cell because the man had bought me for the day. That's all.

I'd been woken up early today. Marcos's men had showered and waxed me, and Marcos had watched. He always watched. He enjoyed being there when people hurt me. But now... now I was somewhere else. Somewhere I'd never been. In a room with carpet instead of the concrete floors that were everywhere in Marcos's complex. It was a real room, not a concrete box with furnishings.

This was a motel. I heard the water running in the bathroom and watched as the door opened. A man wearing a white button up shirt and jeans stepped into the room. He had short black hair, tan skin, and dark eyes. He gave me the half-smile that pretty men tried on me, an instinctual flirtation.

His eyes were cold though, regardless of the smile. This was a man that lived in the same world as Marcos and I did. The boyish charm that didn't quite fit a man in his mid-thirties wasn't enough to convince me that he was the good guy.

"I'm glad you woke up, Maia. I'd thought that you'd have woken up earlier, but I guess I overdid it on the benzos." I didn't answer him. He hadn't asked me a question. Why would he have drugged me? Where was I? Marcos had never let a customer take me out of the compound.

"I hadn't wanted to drug you, but after watching them… do what they did, I knew that you'd never trust me. How could you? I had to get you out of that place."

My mind was still reeling from whatever he'd given me, but had he just told me that he had taken me from Marcos?

He was watching me carefully when he said, "I'm sorry. I haven't introduced myself yet. My name is Angel." His previously almost frantic talking seemed to slow as he gathered himself. Had he been worried?

Maybe he was afraid that he'd killed one of Marcos's slaves.

"Now I just have to get you to the states, and then you can go home to your family." As he talked, his eyes wandered over my body. I'd seen the same thing from so many men that I'd learned the expression. He was taking in my curves and appreciating my body. He talked of saving me, but he still looked at me with the same hunger as every other man.

"I don't have any family," I said.

"Well, I can get you to safety at least. Someplace Marcos can't get you."

I had a million questions, but I knew better than to ask them. He'd tell me what he wanted me to know. Maybe this "rescue" was his game. Maybe he wanted to be someone's hero and then he'd bring me back to Marcos after he was done with his ridiculous fantasy.

"Yes, sir," I said.

He gave me a quizzical look before coming into the room and sitting down on the bed across from me.

"As long as you do what I say, you'll be safe, Maia. It will take a little while to get you out of Mexico. We need to be prepared for the worst which means that Marcos has men looking everywhere for you. I'll have to get you closer to Mexico City before I'll feel comfortable."

"Yes, sir." This man was insane. If he'd really taken me from Marcos, then Marcos would find us soon enough and then he'd kill Angel and punish me. If not, then the best thing I could do would be to do what he said.

Again, he gave me an odd look before saying, "If I untie you, please don't try to run away. Marcos doesn't have any pictures of me, but he'll have plenty of you to spread around. Everyone will be looking for a pale blonde in her teens. I don't want you to end up back with him, and I can't protect you if I'm not there."

"Yes, sir." I hoped for both of our sakes that he was playing a game with me. If he'd actually taken me out of Marcos's compound, he'd doomed us both.

Regardless of my thoughts, Angel untied my bonds. The ropes had been loose. Marcos knew knots. I knew knots. This man didn't. He was quickly making it obvious that he was an idiot. It didn't matter though. He was my customer for the day, and I did what the customer said. Always.

I rubbed my wrists and continued to look at the ground in front of me, never giving him an obvious glance. That puzzled look crossed his face again, but then it was gone, and he stood up.

"What would you like me to do, sir?" I asked.

Angel didn't say anything for a moment as a thought crossed his mind. Then he said, "Sadly, there isn't much to do here in this shitty motel room, but there's a TV if you understand Spanish."

I glanced at the TV, and out of the corner of my eye, I noticed the curtains. They were closed, but a beam of golden light streamed between them. Light I hadn't seen in almost a decade. Sunlight.

Unable to control myself, I looked up at Angel for the first time. None of this made sense. I'd had men that wanted to play games with me. I'd had men that wanted to test me, to see if they could torture me mentally.

None of them had brought me to a place with sunlight though.

My heart beat fiercely, but I'd learned to be patient. I'd learned to control myself, and though most people wouldn't have considered that look to be a break in training, Marcos would have. Quickly, I got control of myself and bowed my head again like a good slave.

"Yes, sir."

"You can lay down in bed if you'd like," he said as he stepped back.

"Yes, sir." I walked to the bed on the other side of the room and laid down with my head on the pillow. Angel tossed me a remote and said, "I'm going to go into town and get some food for us. I'll be back soon."

He grabbed his keys and wallet from the table next to the other bed. With a final glance at me as I stared at the wall, he opened the door and left me in the motel all alone.

I didn't hesitate.

Getting out of bed, I ran to the curtain and peeked out. It was so bright out that it had to have been noon. Or maybe the afternoon. I thought about it for a second and realized that I'd been away from the sun for so long that I barely remembered what it was like. The moon would have probably felt bright to me at this point.

Angel was walking through a parking lot with only a few cars in it to an old blue truck. He had actually taken me away from Marcos. Maybe there were guards waiting at the corners of the motel waiting for me to run out, or maybe he was just an idiot who thought he could get away with stealing from Marcos. It didn't matter.

This was the first chance that I'd ever had to escape from Marcos and the daily torture. Angel might actually be a well-meaning man who thought he was doing a good deed by rescuing me, but he was too stupid to actually keep me safe.

I was the only person that I could trust to keep myself safe. I was the only person in the world who was willing to do whatever it took. I'd find myself a hole in the ground somewhere that I could whore myself out. There was nothing that any man could do that Marcos hadn't already done a hundred times over.

I knew that my body was worth enough for food and rent, and that's all I needed. Hell, I'd be fine even without the roof over my head. Eating and drinking was all I really needed. Even living on the streets in Mexico would be better than Marcos.

My first thought was to race out of the motel room as soon as I saw the truck pull out, but my training held me still. Patience. Daylight was no time for escaping. There would be nowhere to hide, not for an incredibly white girl in Mexico.

I took a few breaths and calmed myself. It would do no good to try to run and immediately get caught. This was my only chance, and it wouldn't be a chance I'd ever get again if I were caught. I needed to do this the right way. Tonight, I would run. Tonight, I would find freedom from the pain of my life, and if I couldn't manage to escape, I would find a way to die.

For now, though, I needed to get some rest. The night would be exhausting. I crawled into the bed and let the blanket envelope me in comfort. It was so soft that I fell asleep almost immediately.

Pain may have been waiting for me after my nap. I could have been woken up at any time with pain, but I always had that. The comfort was new, and it was something to cherish, even if only for a little while. So I rested better than I had in years even though in only a few hours I was going to pit myself against both Angel and Marcos in my escape.

My eyes closed and my breath deepened as sleep came over me while Angel was gone. Almost an hour passed.

The door opened, Angel walked through and quickly closed the door behind him. He carried a bag of food from some sort of restaurant. I sat up, instantly awake again. Smiling, he said, "I didn't know what you would want, so I got you some arrechera tacos. Americans would call them fajitas. Everybody likes fajitas, right? Why don't you come eat some while they're still hot?"

The smell of cooked meat wafted across the room, a scent I barely remembered. Without thinking, without speaking, I crossed the room and sat down in front of the Styrofoam takeout trays. He pushed one to me, and I opened it. It had been so long. So long.

I didn't start eating. Instead, I just sat and smelled the food. My eyes closed instinctively shutting off my other sense so that I could focus on the scent of the food. It was calming and almost blissful.

Then I realized that Angel was staring at me, and I opened my eyes. He was smiling at me. I didn't like the intense focus he was giving me, but that didn't matter much. I didn't like most things in my life. Especially the things that men enjoyed. I picked up a piece of meat, surprised at its warmth. Mush was always room temperature. I put it into my mouth and tried chewing, but it had been a long time, and my jaw and tongue didn't remember exactly what to do.

Slowly, I ate the food, being sure not to bite my tongue or my cheeks even though they seemed to constantly get in the way. Angel kept watching me, like he was enjoying the sight of me eating. What was wrong with him? Had he bought me just so that he could watch me eat?

It didn't matter, though. I would let anyone watch me if they kept feeding me this kind of food. I'd forgotten how much I enjoyed real food. Food with texture and flavor and substance. I had thought that the meat and vegetable mush had been tasty compared to the rest. It was nothing. There is a very good reason normal people didn't eat mush.

Angel pushed a cardboard cup with a straw to me, and I picked it up. I remembered take-out drinks too. I took a sip of the contents and was sure that I made a strange face. It was some sort of soda. I clearly remembered the way that the bubbles popped in my mouth and gave me gas.

It was not my favorite. "Do I have to drink it?" I asked.

"Of course not," he said, his eyebrows drawing closer together. "You don't have to do anything you don't want to do."

I nodded. "Then I would rather not drink this. It's upsetting my stomach."

"Do you like the fajitas?" he asked with a smile. He knew the answer. My face had told him that I'd been in heaven while I ate them, and he just wanted verbal confirmation. Men liked to hear that they'd done well.

"Yes sir. Thank you for the food. I like it," I said.

"I'm glad." He stood up and cleaned up the mess while I watched him. I didn't know what was expected of me or what I was supposed to do.

"What would you like me to do, sir?" I asked. Angel smiled at me and said, "There's not a lot to do, Maia. Mostly, we're just waiting. Just keep breathing free air for now. Like I said before, TV's just about the only thing that we have to entertain ourselves with."

He'd given me food. Real food. This could all be some sort of elaborate plot to hurt me, or he could have rescued me. It didn't matter which because even if Marcos had been the one to give me the food, I would have felt gratitude. My life was all about pain, but little bits of pleasure like this were a fantasy come to life.

"Is there anything you'd like me to do? Like what Marcos would want me to do?" Angel stared at me, and I couldn't tell what he was thinking.

"No Maia. You don't have to have sex with me. I'm not doing this so I can in your pants."

I should have been happy. I should have been glad that he didn't want to hurt me or use my body, but that's all I'd known. It's what my body had grown up knowing.

I did as he said, and I crawled into my bed. The TV played, and I ignored it. It was time to plan, to make decisions. When I left tonight, there wouldn't be time to plan or think. I would have to run and hide and sneak and survive.

Chapter 4: Escape

Hope is a strange thing. It has no more
substance than lights and shadows, and
yet it will provide as much sustenance as
food and drink. Hope is often the
deciding factor in success or failure. And
yet, it is nothing at all.

𝒯he lights had been off for an hour. Angel was a light snorer, and the rhythm of his snores had been steady. He was asleep. Silently, I slipped out of the bed. I still wore the soft cotton dress. No underwear and no shoes. I took a deep breath.

I was not prepared for this escape. I would never be prepared for it. At the same time, this was the first chance I'd ever been close enough to manage an escape. It was time. Marcos would find Angel soon enough.

Angel was too afraid to hide in the darkest of holes. There was nothing anyone could do to me that was worse than Marcos. Even death was a kindness compared to going back to Marcos. I would survive though. I'd lived too long in pain to need a respite from it.

I slipped out of the door and into the night. A full moon and a cloudless sky watched from above as my bare feet kicked up dust as I ran. I needed distance. I needed a hideaway for the daylight hours.

I thought about trying to do something with a car, but I'd never driven before, much less tried to steal one. No, I would have to run away. I needed to find a village somewhere with barely anyone. I'd cut my hair and dye it. I'd work in the sun to get a tan. Maybe get some wrinkles. Anything to make it to where I didn't fit the description Marcos's men had for me.

I turned down an alley, always staying in the shadows and moving as silently as possible. The last thing I needed was to lure a random drunk to me. The fear of a rape was nothing compared to the fear of lost time. I needed to be far away before the sun came up.

My lungs burned, but I kept running. My feet ached from running barefoot, but I kept running. Pain was such an unimportant thing once your mind realized it. The danger to me was not from a lack of oxygen or cut and bruised feet. It was a man who could find far more ingenious ways to torture a woman.

The road led out of town, and I kept running, but the sun was coming up. I'd been running for hours now. I looked around me. Mesquite bushes grew behind barbed wire fences. Brush that no one cared about, that no one would want to dig through.

I smiled. This was a safe place. As safe as I would find at least. I was careful as I climbed the fence, not wanting to get hung up on the barbs.

I crawled into the brush, not worrying about the small scratches that the mesquite thorns made on my pale skin. When I felt completely covered by the brush, I rested. I was in the shade and wouldn't need to worry about being sunburned.

Hours passed in the heat of the day. I dozed, never sleeping deeply, but not worrying too much about the passing noises. I was hidden well enough.

Nothing changed. Cars and trucks passed. People passed. Donkeys passed. Time passed.

And every minute that passed was a blessing. It was another minute of freedom. Of sunshine on my skin. Of fresh air. Of life. I let the minutes pass without any rush. In truth, I didn't expect to survive outside of Marcos's grasp for long.

He was too cruel, too strong, too terrible. He'd catch me eventually, and I would go back to Hell. And I would find a way to die there. For now, I would revel in the light of the sun and the fresh air even if I were hidden under a mesquite tree.

Grasshoppers buzzed in the brush with me, and I listened to their songs as they jumped and flew, their wings fluttering. Birds chirped and sang as they chased the grasshoppers and other bugs. Sounds that I hadn't heard in so long that I'd forgotten them.

Then I felt something sting my foot. I looked back at my leg and saw fire ants crawling over me. A line of the red insects the size of a grain of rice had formed and would lead back to their ant mound somewhere further in the brush.

Panic instantly filled my mind. It was early afternoon. People were all over the road. It was not a huge city that I could get lost in. People would notice a pretty white girl who obviously hadn't seen the sun in a long time. But the ants were going to kill me. They thought that I wasn't able to walk. I'd seen baby birds that had been eating alive by them when I was a child.

To the ants, I was no different than the baby bird that had fallen from the nest. Easy food. I could either die to the ants or risk being caught. If it had been a choice between being stung for the next few hours and risk being caught, I would have chosen the ants, but I wasn't going to die from ant bites.

I crawled out from the brush and wiped the ants away from my legs knocking them to the ground. Hiding in the brush anywhere on these roads would end up with the same situation. The ants were everywhere out here. I remembered these bastards from when I was a child. I'd completely forgotten them in my plan.

I would have to do something different, and I had only one thing to trade for what I needed.

I climbed the fence and stood on the road smiling at the men driving by in their trucks and cars. A man in a little white car pulled up next to me. He was in his late forties and all smiles as he looked out of his rolled down window.

"Hola, señorita. Entiendes el español?" I shook my head.

He nodded. "My English is not so good," he said in a very heavy Mexican accent. "Are you needing a ride?" he asked.

I nodded and pointed north, down the road. "I need to go to the next town."

The man raised his eyebrows at this and said, "You do not want to go that way. Nothing is that way." He turned and pointed south. "That way is Monterrey. Much better place for una chica bonita like you."

I shook my head. "No. That way," I said, pointing away from Monterrey. The last thing I wanted was to get into a major town. That was probably where Marcos's complex was.

"I am not going that way, señorita. I am going to Monterrey."

I took a deep breath and said, "I can pay, señor." I cupped my pussy and smiled. He raised his eyebrow and said, "Get in señorita. We will talk." I walked around to the other side of his car and opened the door.

He put the car into gear and turned around, heading the way I had pointed. He was quiet which was surprising. After we'd gone several miles down the road, he turned off onto a dirt road. I assumed it was for privacy while he used me.

He turned the car off, and he got out of the car. He pulled a cell phone out of his pocket, and my heart sank. He pointed it at me, and I saw the flash of the camera. He was one of Marcos's men.

I opened the door and tried to run, but he wrapped his fingers around my arm and held me tight. I turned to him and began to kick and punch at him. For a few moments, I lost myself trying to escape.

I was too small and too weak though. The man just wrapped his body around mine. "Hush, hush," he said. "It will be okay."

I didn't stop struggling, but the man didn't stop holding me to him either. We were both committed. If he had told his boss about me, and then he lost me, they'd probably kill him. If I didn't get away, I would experience far worse than death.

I kicked backward, trying to get his balls, but I missed. "Señorita, you must stop trying to hurt me, or I will have to hurt you." He didn't understand. No one could understand the difference between him and what waited for me.

I leaned forward and bit down on his hand, tasting the metallic taste of blood. I felt the flesh begin to tear, and he let go, desperate for the pain in his hand to end, and I rushed forward. I only made it three steps before I felt electricity course through my body.

I fell to the ground shaking as the taser pumped thousands of volts of current through me, shutting my muscles down. It hurt, but more than the pain, it stopped me.

The electricity felt like it coursed through me for ten minutes, but in reality, it probably only ran for a few seconds. Then the nameless man stepped over my body and sat down on me.

"El Jefe will be here soon enough, señorita. I am sorry that I had to call him, but they would kill me if they found out that I hadn't."

I knew what they'd do. I also knew what waited for me if they found me. I gritted my teeth and pushed against the man's weight, hoping that I could roll him off me. I couldn't though. There was nothing that I could do.

And so we waited. And I cried. For the first time in as long as I could remember, I cried. My tears fell down my cheeks and dust curled up from the desert ground where they landed.

A truck pulled in behind us, and I couldn't see anything. I didn't need to see him to know who it was.

"Good evening, Maia. Have you enjoyed your vacation?"

Chapter 5: Slave

Terror is a living thing. A creature with teeth and fangs that devours its victims slowly and constantly. Their very essence fades as it feeds even as the body lives unharmed. A shell is left where a soul once rested.

The ropes were tighter than normal as I looked up at Marcos. I lay on the wooden table, tied in a star position, totally naked once again. Marcos had taken his time building up to this moment.

He'd started easily enough. I'd been forced to service the man who had caught me. Each of my holes had been violated. That was nothing new, and though it was unpleasant, it was not a punishment.

That had been the man's reward. Marcos always rewarded the ones that served him well. Except me. I didn't get rewards even though I had done my best to serve him in any way that he requested.

Marcos had bent me over in the back of the car, and he had pulled out his knife. Without restraining me, he had pressed the blade of the knife against my ass. The sharp sting of my flesh being cut raced through me, but I stayed still.

The blood had run down my legs onto the seat. Marcos didn't seem to care. Slowly, he had taken his time cutting my ass, and I hadn't moved at all. It had hurt, but it was a small pain in comparison to some of the possibilities.

I had watched through the window as we drove back to the town that Angel had stayed in. Marcos must have been excited to get started as he didn't continue on towards whatever city held his complex. Instead, the driver of the car had pulled into a warehouse parking lot.

Marcos had timed the cutting to be finished when we had pulled up to the warehouse. He pulled out his phone and took a picture, showing me his crimson artwork. Long thin red lines crisscrossed my skin. It didn't matter. Even though Angel had meant well, he'd never have been able to keep me safe. At least maybe he wouldn't be killed. He'd been nice enough, and he'd let me have my first taste of real food.

And now I lay on this table looking up at Marcos. "Sweetheart," he said, "why'd you run away from me?"

"I didn't, sir. I was taken from you. You know I could never leave you on my own." He hummed as he looked at something next to him.

"Then why didn't you try to find me? And why did you bite Santiago like some kind of animal when he tried to bring you back to me? Did you want to be with someone other than me?"

He knew that I hated him. That didn't matter though. He didn't want me to say that. That wasn't part of the acting that he expected. I was a slave. "No, sir. I was afraid that he was taking me farther away from you."

"That makes sense, Maia. You have to understand how angry I was when I learned that you'd left though."

"Yes sir," I said, knowing that a punishment was coming.

"And that I'm going to stay angry until you've made me feel better, right?" I nodded. That was the only answer.

"Good," he said with that damned wicked smile. He picked up the thing that he'd been looking at. A branding iron. It was red hot.

My pulse raced. I couldn't keep myself under control.

"Please, sir. Please don't hurt me like this. Please." I pulled at the bindings that held me in place.

"I'm sorry, Maia. This is the only way. It's just another way to remember what you are," he said as he showed me the letters that would soon be burnt into my skin forever.

"SLAVE".

That would be on me forever, for all of the men that would use my body to see. Marcos smiled as he held the iron vertically over my crotch and he slowly lowered it down.

The pain wasn't instant like I thought it would be. Instead, the first thing that let me know that the metal had touched me was the sound. A sizzling, like a steak had been put on a hot griddle. Then the pain flashed through me like electricity, and I screamed and writhed on the table.

"That's it, Maia. Take the pain," he said.

He continued to hold the red-hot iron to my skin for what seemed like forever. I screamed and screamed, and out of nowhere, I felt an orgasm build inside of me and explode outward.

"That's a good girl," Marcos said as he pulled the metal away from my skin. I looked down at my mound. The flesh still smoked from where the metal had burnt the word into me.

I should have been crying. A normal girl would have still been screaming and destroyed. Not me. No, I was just noticing how there was a wet spot under my ass where I'd cum so hard that I'd squirted. From being branded.

It hurt. Everything hurt, but the pain didn't matter. Only the realization that I was never going to stop being a slave. Marcos had broken me permanently. He was already putting a salve on the brand, and I didn't make a sound as he put a bandage over it.

A tear rolled down my cheek as I accepted that I would never be free of this man or this life. Only death would save me from it.

That's when I heard the gunshot. Then another. I jerked to the side, and Marcos wasn't there. I couldn't see him. What had happened? I picked my head up and saw Angel running towards me, a pistol in his hand as he glanced around the warehouse.

"Are you okay, Maia?" he said hurriedly. He glanced down at the bandage above my pussy, and he grimaced.

"I'm fine, Angel. What are you doing here? Where did Marcos go?" My eyes were wild. Everything about me was wild right then.

"He's lying on the ground dead, Maia. Same with the driver." He pulled out a knife and quickly cut the ropes that bound me. I looked over the side. I had to see him. Had to see the bastard that had spent nearly a decade torturing me for no reason. I had to be sure that he was dead.

He lay on the ground, unmoving as a river of blood slowly moved towards the table. A dark red stain around a hole in his nice dress shirt. The memory of my mother looking the same way echoed in my mind, and I smiled.

"Come on, Maia. There were other guards outside. We have to go. Now." His voice was filled with fear and need. I jumped down, wincing as the brand shot electric pain through me.

He led me out of the building, running as fast as we could. As soon as we got out of the building, I heard gunshots, and Angel yanked the door to his truck open. He pushed me inside and slammed the door before running to his side. He hadn't even gotten his door shut before the truck was started and he was racing away from the warehouse.

I looked behind me and two men holding rifles aimed at us. I saw the flash from the guns as they began to unload in our direction. Angel swerved on the road as the shots continued, but then they were gone.

He didn't slow down though, and I didn't say anything. Marcos was dead.

I looked at Angel. His eyes were wild now. His motions were erratic, but he was still in control. He'd killed the man who had ruined my life. He'd rid the world of the worst monster I'd ever known.

And he'd saved me. Again.

Maybe I could trust him after all. My mind flashed to Marcos again. Flashed to the pool of blood that had turned into a river. Dead. He'd never hurt me again. I put my hand over the bandage, felt the swollen flesh beneath it and smiled. I wasn't upset about the brand anymore. It may say slave, but it meant freedom.

The last thing that he ever did was give me this mark. Only a minute sooner, and I would have remained unblemished with nothing but normal scars to remind me of the time that I was his.

The truck flew down the road, hitting curves faster than he should have and passing any vehicle that got in his way. He continued north, away from Monterrey, and I laid my head back. Angel was taking me away from the pain. He hadn't been lying.

Chapter 6: Clean

The webs bound them together, a mass of
silky strands of silver. Each memory a
twisting knot of ether. Always invisible,
but undeniable. These tethers bound
them, and only the flames that raged
inside had the strength to release them.

Maia was sleeping finally. After she'd run, I'd
been forced to find her. It was a good thing that I had
a lot of experience in finding people who don't want to
be found. It was also good that I'd expected her to
run.

She hadn't believed me when I'd said that I could
protect her. How could she believe anything after what
she'd gone through? She'd been a slave when I'd taken
her, and that hadn't changed just because I said some
words to her.

Now, well now she trusted me at least a little.
Marcos wouldn't hurt her again. That seemed to make
all the difference.

She looked peaceful this time. Not like in the motel. That had been relaxing, not sleeping. I took a deep breath. She was beautiful when she smiled. Her body was gorgeous, even with all the scars. No one who knew her could call the scars imperfections. They'd been the fire that had forged a woman strong enough to survive Marcos and his compound.

I shivered when I thought about the hell that she'd been put through. That was done though. As long as she listened to me, I would be able to keep her safe. That was something that I knew that I could do.

She was curled up in the bed next to me. Damn villages never had normal accommodations. This motel only had rooms with king-sized beds left, and Maia didn't have any clothes. This was not how I had planned things. Not at all.

I could have gone out and bought something for her, but she needed me here, and she didn't seem to be shy about her nudity in the slightest. I guess that happens when you don't wear clothes for half your life.

The fan continued its slow spinning, and the blanket slid down Maia's body as she tried to get out from under the heat. Sweat glistened on her alabaster skin. She was the most beautiful woman I'd ever seen. Only nineteen years old.

And I couldn't touch her. I couldn't be another monster for her to deal with. No, I wouldn't push her into anything.

I tried to turn over in the bed in an attempt to get her out of my mind, but I couldn't manage to get the girl out of my mind enough to sleep. Finally, I got out of bed and walked to the bathroom. Using my hand as a cup, I took a few drinks of water from the faucet. I took some deep breaths and looked in the mirror, trying to convince myself silently to relax and to stop thinking about her.

It didn't work. Instead, thoughts of what I would have done to her if I'd just been a customer ran through my mind. I was a monster, just like Marcos. The only difference was where our evil lay, and for me, this girl was over the line. I didn't want her to see the dark sides of me.

I didn't act on my desires, but I had to do something to push my body away from lust. I walked out of the bathroom and started doing pushups. Physical exertion had helped in the past. If I exhausted myself, maybe it would be enough to let me get at least a little shut eye.

When I felt like I couldn't do even one more pushup, I looked up to see Maia staring down at me on the floor.

"Why are you doing that?" she asked quietly.

"I'm having a hard time sleeping," I replied. It was hard to look at her without letting my eyes roam over her naked body that she did absolutely nothing to cover up.

"Why?" she asked.

I took a deep breath. "I'm having trouble getting my mind to stop thinking." She nodded at this comment and I breathed a little easier.

"That happens sometimes when I know that I'm going to be hurt really badly. It was hard to sleep the night before you stole me from Marcos because he said that you were going to hurt me more than normal."

"I wonder why he said that?" she said as the thought came. "Are you going to hurt me? Is that why you stole me from Marcos? Because you knew that I'm broken the way that men like?"

I turned away. I'd said something along those lines, but it had been mostly a lie. All the best lies are based on truth, though. I'd wanted her in all the ways that I could never let her see. I'd watched as the man had beaten her, had watched as she'd cum over and over again, and regardless of how terrible I felt for her, the sight had made me want her even more.

"No, Maia. I will never make you do anything. Never. You're not a slave, and if you decided that you wanted to walk out that door, I wouldn't stop you. It would be a bad decision, but I wouldn't stop you." I scooted back to the wall and leaned against it, putting some distance between the two of us.

"Why don't you want to hurt me? Everyone else does." She wasn't angry. She was just curious.

"I don't want you to do anything that you don't want to do. I've done a lot of bad things in my life, but I've never forced a woman into bed with me."

Maia seemed to think about this for a few moments before saying, "Thank you for rescuing me from Marcos, sir. Thank you for saving me."

"You're welcome. I'm sorry that I couldn't take you away sooner." She shrugged.

"It's done. The pain is gone, and the scars don't hurt. Maybe one day I may even have a real life, but for now, I'm just happy that I will never have to see Marcos again." There was real joy in her eyes, and I was glad to see it.

"About Marcos," I said, knowing that I was pulling the joy out of a midnight conversation. "He may be gone, but the organization he worked for isn't. Until we get across the border, they're going to be looking for us."

Surprisingly, Maia smiled. "Yes, but if they find us, they'll kill us. I was prepared to die. Death is nothing compared to being sent back to Marcos's compound. Nothing anyone can do will be as bad as being sent back there."

I didn't really understand how she could say that, but I could never understand the pain and suffering she'd endured. "I would rather not die, though, so I need you to listen to me. I have smuggled things through Mexican cartel lines plenty of times, and this is no different. You just have to trust that I know what I'm doing."

Maia nodded. "I trust you. You got me away from them twice now. Just tell me what to do, and I'll do it."

I smiled and shook my head. It was hard to keep myself from telling her all of the things that I wanted her to do, all of the things that I could never tell her to do.

"For now, we need to just sit tight in the room for the next three days," I said.

"Okay. We'll sleep and watch TV and rest. I could use some rest. It's been a long life," she said with a smile.

I nodded and stood up. She looked at me with the same confused look in her eyes that she'd had when I'd gotten into bed the first time.

"What?" I asked.

"Aren't you hot in all those clothes?" she asked, and I had a hard time not giving her a snide comment, but she was right. I was covered in sweat from wearing my pants, boxers, and a shirt in a room without air conditioning.

"Yes, but I'm worried about what I'll do if I'm not wearing all these clothes. It would be a lot different if there were two beds."

She shook her head. "I won't be angry if you do something, Angel. I don't know if I could be angry with you for anything."

I just stared at her. She made things so difficult. Laying there naked and telling me she wouldn't be angry if I fucked her. I had to take several very deep breaths.

"I'll take my pants and shirt off, but I'm keeping my boxers on," I said resolutely.

"Yes sir," she said softly, shrugged, and then turned around to face the closed door. I looked at her body, at her naked back as the sheet only covered half her ass. I struggled with my desires, but I still stripped off the button up shirt and jeans before crawling into bed.

The exercise had helped. Sore muscles always helped me to relax when my mind wouldn't listen. It didn't take long to fall asleep.

Once I was asleep, it didn't take long for my desires to take over.

Chapter 7: Desperation

She walked a road that another had built. Thorns with dark crimson tips rose from the edges, and her only choice was to go on. No matter how dark the road became, she could never turn back. Not now, not ever.

I felt it before I was awake, but I didn't act on it. I'd never acted sexually without direction. He was so hard, though. He thrust against my back, and I could feel the wet spot on his boxers. I'd never enjoyed sex. No matter how many orgasms I'd had, I'd never enjoyed them. Yet, for some reason, I felt the desire to please him.

I tried to remind myself that he wasn't Marcos. He wasn't a bad man. He was just a man, and men needed to use women's bodies. It was the way that the world worked.

I'd been trained for it. My entire life had revolved around satisfying men's needs. Maybe he wouldn't even hurt me. Even if he hurt me, I knew that he wouldn't hurt me like Marcos. No one would ever hurt me like him, and that was all because of Angel.

He'd saved me. He'd killed the man who had ruined my life. He'd done it all without an ounce of payment from me. I could do this for him. It cost me nothing, but it would make him feel better. It would satisfy the hunger he had inside him, the hunger that all men silently but constantly fought against.

I reached behind me, and I felt his hard cock. I wrapped my fingers around it through his boxers, and I squeezed him. He moaned, and I could feel myself getting wet already.

I turned around and looked at Angel sleeping. I didn't know what to do. I didn't know what he wanted or even if he wanted me at all. Maybe he was dreaming about another woman. Or maybe a man.

No, I'd seen him looking at me like he wanted to use me. He wanted to use me just like the other men had. I just didn't know how. "Angel," I said softly, nervously.

His eyes opened, and he moaned as I squeezed his cock. "Do you like this?" I asked.

"Mmmhmmm," he moaned, barely awake. I reached my hand into his boxers and gripped his cock without the boxers in the way, and he moaned again.

I stroked him, and he began to thrust into my hand. He wanted more. He wanted to be inside of me.

I pulled his boxers down and climbed on top of him. Straddling his thighs, I looked down at him before I began to lower myself onto him.

And for the first time in my life, I decided to feel a man inside of me. No one forced me. No one ordered me. This was my idea, and for some reason that mattered so much more than I'd ever thought it would.

And nothing hurt. In fact, as I rode Angel's cock, pleasure began to shoot through my body. His hands ran over my body, never holding me tightly, never pushing me to do anything, just letting me fuck him how I wanted. Up and down, up and down.

His eyes watched my body, enjoying the way that I moved without any need to change it. He'd wanted to see me like this from the very beginning. He could have said anything, but I knew that he'd wanted me on top of him from the first time he saw me.

"You're beautiful," he said. I didn't respond with words. He didn't need them. Instead, I ran my hands over his chest and felt the soft hair run between my fingers.

Angel's hands moved to my breasts, gently cupping them. His large hands were warm and so soft, and the sensations coursed through my body, making me finally understand how a woman might want sex.

This was different than anything I'd ever felt. Different from every other time I'd had sex. The choice made all the difference. The actions may have been the same, but that simple choice turned it into something that I could enjoy.

"You... Fuck that feels good..." I smiled at him. Men had complimented me before, but none had felt like this when they were doing it. None had been grateful. They'd seen me as a toy to be enjoyed, but Angel viewed me as a woman that was doing something for him of her own free will.

I stopped bouncing and began to grind on him. More pleasure ran through me, and I finally let out a moan. I had no idea that sex could feel like. Was this how it felt for the men that had used my body?

Angel's hand drifted higher, and his fingers wrapped around my throat. He didn't put any pressure on me. He just moved his fingers over my skin as he had done with the rest of my body, but I felt the need begin to rise.

An orgasm was stirring inside me, and I felt like I wanted to cry. How could I be so broken? Maybe it would be different with Angel. Maybe I could be more than the broken doll that Marcos had turned me into.

My body moved faster, and with more roughness. His cock was big enough. It should hurt more. I needed it to hurt more. But it didn't. It couldn't. I wanted it too badly. I was too willing.

His fingers traced my jaw, and I felt the orgasm building inside me. I felt the wall too, the wall that would keep it bottled up.

"You make me feel so good, Maia. So fucking good." His words didn't help me. There was nothing cruel in them. Nothing hurtful.

Maybe he could draw the orgasm out. Maybe he could be the one to break a lifetime of training. Maybe I just couldn't fuck good enough.

I sat up and smiled at him, knowing not to let my despair show. No man wanted to see a girl who was sad. That had been trained into me.

I got on my hands and knees and turned to Angel. "Please fuck me," I said. I tried to be seductive, but truthfully, I was desperate. I wouldn't be able to keep that away from his gaze. He seemed to see everything.

He nodded and sat up, positioning himself behind me. I looked at the wall, preparing for the pain. He slipped inside me effortlessly. No pain.

And it felt so good. Amazingly good. Perfectly good. So fucking frustratingly good.

His hands gripped my hips and he began to use me how he wanted to. He wasn't gentle with my body, but my body and mind were so broken and messed up that it didn't hurt. In fact, everything still felt incredible.

And the orgasm continued to build behind the wall of training inside of me. Building and growing. Angel would never understand this part of me.

I felt his rhythm building into a crescendo. Grunting and moaning from Angel. The sound of flesh slapping flesh stopped, and a sadness filled me. The orgasm was still there trapped behind the wall. It wouldn't go away for a long time. The need and desperation wouldn't leave me. Not until it was released through pain.

Angel slid to the bed beside me with a smile on his face. He was pleased and content at least. I smiled back at him and rolled off the bed to go to the bathroom and clean up.

This was the cruelest thing that Marcos had done. He'd built a box inside of me where all orgasms hid, and the only key was my own pain. It didn't matter what I did, release would never come for me until I experienced pain. The bigger the orgasm built, the more intense the pain would need to be.

I ran my hand lightly over the bandage that covered my brand, feeling the raised skin that was covered in small scabs. Even the brand wasn't as cruel. Especially now that I knew that Marcos would never hurt me again. That training was still hurting me though. It might hurt me forever while the pain behind the brand would heal quickly enough.

I walked back into the bedroom and looked at Angel laying on the bed with a smile on his face. The thin sheen of sweat covered his naked body, and I wanted him. I wouldn't be fucking him next time because he needed it. I'd be doing it because I wanted it, because I needed him.

I just hoped that the next time was soon because the orgasm hidden inside me was making me desperate already.

"That wasn't what I'd expected to wake up to," Angel said. I forced a smile, trying to hide the need.

"You wanted it, and I wanted to say thank you with more than words." I looked down at the ground, unsure about whether I'd done the right thing.

"That's a hell of a thank you. I hope you enjoyed it too."

"I..." I stopped for a moment, unsure of how to phrase my thoughts. "I liked it. A lot."

He smiled at me. "Well, you can do that anytime you're in the mood," he said with a bit of a chuckle. "But I'm going to have a hard time not running my hands over that sexy little body of yours more often," he said.

That comment made me blush a little bit, and I stared at the ground again. He wasn't one of Marcos's customers. I cared what Angel thought about me.

He stood up and walked across the room to me. He put his hand under my chin and pulled my head up to look at him. "None of that, Maia. I know that they trained you to act like that. I don't want you to do it anymore. They're gone. They're dead. You don't have to do anything that they trained you to do. Never again."

If only he understood. It wasn't training. It was building. They'd broken me, and they'd crushed the pieces. Then they'd molded the pieces into someone new. I wasn't the Maia that my mother had known. I was the Maia that Marcos had built. If I stopped doing what they'd trained me to do, I would be nothing.

"Yes... Angel," I said. He nodded.

"That's a good start. Now, what do you want to do today?" he asked with a happy grin.

I glanced down at his cock, and he raised an eyebrow. "You'll probably have to give me a little bit before I'll be ready to go again," he said.

"Will you let me try?" I said softly as I looked into his eyes.

"Go for it. I just know my body is all," he said with another grin. "But I'm never going to complain about a sexy girl wanting my cock."

I smiled and dropped to me knees in front of him. The feel of the carpet on my knees was strange. All I'd ever known was hard concrete. This was luxurious. I could kneel for Angel for hours if he wanted it.

I reached my hands around his thighs to grip his ass, and I swallowed his cock. Without a bit of resistance, I let it slip down my throat and looked up at him. The shock in his eyes was apparent, and I could feel it swelling in my throat already.

I bobbed on it, using his ass to pull myself to him. "Fuck," he breathed as my tongue tickled the bottom of his cock while I swallowed him. When I let him go, I smiled up at him as we both looked at his very hard cock covered in my spit. This was what I'd been made for.

"I won't doubt your magical powers ever again. I promise," he said as he picked me up and threw me onto the bed.

Chapter 8: Anything

He consumed the very life that she radiated, drinking in her essence. And he glowed in the darkness. She was slowly dying, but the light that he gave her filled her with joy and was the most beautiful thing she'd ever seen. Would it be kinder to force her to live in darkness forever or to allow her to see the light until she died?

"Remember, when we get into town, you have to hide. No one can see you. There will be pictures of you circulating, but there won't be any of me," Angel said with a smile.

It was hard to look at him. We'd spent the past three days fucking and resting and talking, in that order. I hadn't cum even once. The sex had been wonderful, but the little bubble of desperation hidden behind the wall of training had grown into a monster of need.

I tried not to let my mind run to thoughts of pain and agony. I didn't want that to be a part of me anymore. I wanted to be something more human than whatever I'd become. I wasn't a slave anymore. I didn't have to follow my training anymore, and some of it was falling away.

I didn't say "sir" very much now. I looked Angel in the eyes more and more without the fear of being hit. I even initiated sex.

The only piece of my training was that still completely whole was that damned wall. I still couldn't cum, and my mind and body were desperate for the release.

"We have to move away from the border. There are a lot more cartel members that patrol these major border routes, and they will all be looking for you. So instead, we'll slowly make our way to Veracruz where we'll hide out for a month or so. Finally, after things have calmed down enough, I'll get us on a boat headed to Florida, and we'll be free then."

He seemed so sure of his plan, so confident in his ability to get us out of the cartel's grasp. I had thought that Marcos was the one who was ruining my life, but it seemed that the Sinaloa Cartel did this regularly in many places. Marcos was just the leader of the compound that I had been brought to. Broken whores who were available for any kind of use were a high paying business.

"Why don't we just find a boat to Florida in a few days?" I asked.

"Because all the ports have Cartel members watching them. Even the one in Veracruz. I killed a high-ranking member, so they're out for blood. We need to let something else catch their attention before we try to get out of Mexico."

I nodded. "Where did you learn all this stuff?"

"I'm not the good guy, Maia. I've probably hurt more people than Marcos has. I just haven't hurt them the same way. I'm a smuggler. It doesn't matter what someone wants to move, I can get it there. Whether that's drugs or cars or weapons."

"Or people," I said softly.

He nodded. "Or people. I've never tortured a woman for my own pleasure before, Maia, but I have tortured women before. And men. And even children."

The Mexican desert raced by us as the truck threw up dust. I looked out the open window with a sigh.

"Is that why you met with Marcos? Why you bought me? You wanted to torture me?" I didn't look at Angel. I couldn't. I didn't want to think about him like that.

He put his hand on my thigh, and I pulled away for the first time. He let me go, and he said, "No. I thought that Marcos ran a whorehouse. I didn't know that he ran a slave training facility. I just thought I would go and get my dick wet in a sexy Mexican whore."

He paused for a moment, letting his words settle in the air. "And then I saw you. And I couldn't let him treat you that way. I'm a terrible person. I don't get upset when bad things happen to good people, but what he was doing to you was beyond what I could handle. I couldn't let it happen anymore. That's why I bought you. That's why I rescued you. That's why I put myself in the crosshairs of the Sinaloa Cartel for you.

"So you're going to keep hurting people?" I asked, just a tiny bit of hope beginning to grow inside of me.

"Yes. I didn't say that I used to be a bad person. I didn't say that I'd changed. What I'm doing for you isn't me changing. It's a… it's a fucking stupid decision because for some really messed up reason, I don't want anyone to do anything to you that you don't want."

I took a deep breath and let it out slowly. Before I could say anything, he continued, "And that's why I'm *not* going to try to convince you to be with me. Maia, you're incredible. Everything a man could want. But I'm not the man you should be with. I'm not the man anyone should be with."

"We can keep fucking and having fun during these escapades in Mexico, but I don't want you to have any thoughts about staying with me afterward. I'd only bring you more heartache. It's all I do."

I nodded to him and looked out the window. I didn't want to think about all the bad things that he could have done. Instead, I turned my mind towards the future and wondered what I would do when I was finally free of Mexico, when I was free of the world I'd lived in for so long. What did people do? I only had one skill, and I didn't want to go from one hell to another one.

"What are you thinking, Maia?" Angel asked, giving me a quick glance before turning back to the road.

"I don't know. Just... Being a slave was simple. It was terrible and horrible, and I never want to go back to it, but it was simple. Now, I have to think about things like what I'm going to do when I'm free. That's hard on everyone, I'm sure. I know that lots of kids in school talked about what they wanted to be when they grew up."

"But it's more than that. I have to think about what to eat. I love the fact that I get to eat all these wonderful foods, but sometimes, it might be easier to just not have to think about it, to not have to make those little decisions. Sometimes, maybe not having the choices is easier."

I quickly added, "I'm not ungrateful, Angel. I promise. This is better. It's just different, and I'm not used to thinking about things or being in charge of even the simple parts of my life that everyone else is used to. Maybe that's why I like having sex. At least that's something I know. I'm not afraid or nervous when it comes to sex. I don't have to think about it."

I looked at Angel, and he just stared ahead, his brow furrowed in thought. "What if I didn't make you think about the simple things? What if I just picked the food, and you ate it?" he asked.

I grinned and laughed a little. "That'd be wonderful. It's more than just the food, though. You know that. It's all the little things. What do I want to watch on TV? What do I want to wear?" I looked at the bag that held my limited supply of extra clothes. Normal people had to have clothes. Sadly.

"Right now, there's not very much to decide, but when I get back to the normal world, I don't know whether I'll be able to handle all the decisions. I definitely don't know if I can remember all the things that most people remember. And how am I going to learn how to live on my own fast enough?"

"Those are just things that you'll have to deal with when they come up. Everyone does. You'll be able to do it. If you can survive hell and still smile, I'm positive that you'll be able to handle paying bills and working at a grocery store. You'll learn how to do all those little things that scare you, and I'll help you out. I wouldn't take you to America only to drop you off penniless. That'd be almost as bad as leaving you in Mexico."

No, it wouldn't. I knew that I could fuck and suck my way through life. I was nineteen. I was pretty. People would pay plenty to have access to just an hour of my body. Especially if I was okay with them doing more than the other whores. Marcos had made plenty of money off my body. More than enough to pay for a roof, and clothes, and food. And I'd get to choose what I did and for whom I did it.

"Thank you, Angel. For everything. I wish that I could do more for you." He glanced at me and a chill ran down my spine. He was a bad man. A man who had done terrible things to people, and I could see that evil behind his eyes. For just a split-second, he looked like the men that had used me before.

"Your smile is enough, Maia. I would have done the same thing even if I'd never seen you again."

The smile I gave him was a little more forced than usual. It was hard to forget the hint of my past on his face, but I tried to remind myself that he was *my* hero regardless of the pain he inflicted on others. There were good men, but I'd never met one. Maybe all I could hope for was an evil man that was good to *me*.

Unlike the good men out there, the men who worked in offices and wore suits to work, this man could protect me from the rest of the evil in the world. He could fight them. He could kill them. He *had* killed them.

That realization hit me hard. I could never have a nice man. I could never have a gentle man. Those kinds of people would die when the evil came looking for me. Just like my mother. She'd been kind and she'd been gentle. And she was dead because of it.

I looked at Angel again, really looked at him, and I saw that evilness inside him. I'd seen it before. Flashes of it crossed his face regularly even though he tried to hide it from me. I'd tried to ignore it. It was the reason I'd run away initially. It was the reason that Marcos was dead and I was free.

Angel was a villain in this story, and I was glad of it.

Chapter 9: Freedom

*She loved his light, but she couldn't
survive without his darkness.*

This motel was nicer. Much nicer actually. It had a working refrigerator, and the walls had nice wallpaper on them. There wasn't any dust in the room, and the maids came every day. We didn't let them into the room, of course, but they would have come if we'd let them. It even came with a few bottles of liquor.

There had been rooms with two queens, but I'd asked for a single King. Angel had smiled at that, and I'd liked the way he'd looked at me. That lusty look he'd given me initially had softened now that he knew that I was his to play with. At least until we got to Florida. I wondered if it would make him get us there slower. Then I wondered if I wanted him to hurry us out of Mexico.

The real world was scary, but it was the thing that waited for me when we got to Florida. Until then, it was just lazy naked days and nights spent with Angel, enjoying takeout that he got for us and terrible Mexican television.

And that desperate need that grew every day. A need that threatened to consume me. I was wet all day, every day now. His touch made me shake a little. Nothing would break that wall of training down, though.

"What do you want for dinner?" Angel asked. I shrugged my shoulders. I didn't care. Food had lost its flavor at this point. I only had enough room in my mind for one kind of hunger.

"How about some chicken?" He put his shirt on. A blue button up shirt that he tucked into his jeans.

"I don't care, Angel. I don't even think I'm hungry," I said. I sat in the bed, still naked.

"What's wrong?" he asked as he sat down on the bed next to me. "You're always so excited to try new food. What's going on?"

"Nothing," I said quietly as I kept staring at the wall.

He reached out and put his hand on my knee, and I started shivering softly. *If only he'd grab me harder. Spread my legs whether I wanted him to or not. Slap my pussy hard enough to make me scream. That's what I needed.*

"Maia, please tell me what's wrong. You've been…" he took a breath and thought for a moment, "different. Did I do something?"

I'd tried to hide it, tried to let the pressure building inside me break that damned wall down. It wasn't working though. Nothing was working. I needed the pressure to be released. I desperately needed relief.

I gave up. "I'm fucked up, Angel. Marcos broke me." I turned to look at him. "I haven't cum since we started having sex. I haven't gone twelve hours without cumming in my adult life, and now I've gone four days of constant sex without an orgasm."

Angel looked down at the bed instead of at me. Shamefully, he sat there in front of me with a defeated look on his face, and it occurred to me that he didn't understand what I was saying.

"That's not what I meant, Angel. You didn't do anything wrong." I sighed as I was forced to deal with his emotions instead of being able to focus on my own. "Angel, I was trained to only cum from being hurt. You could fuck me like a god, but until you hurt me, I would never cum."

"What?" he asked as he looked up with at least a little bit of relief in his expression. That relief only frustrated me.

"I cannot orgasm without pain. It was a huge part of how I was... *built*," I said. That was truer than training would have been. Training was something you did for a dog. And it certainly wasn't something you did for eight years.

"Maia, are you telling me that you want me to hurt you?" he asked, and I took a deep breath. I had wanted to keep this part of me a secret. I'd wanted to keep it secret until it wasn't real anymore, until it just went away. That didn't seem like it was possible though.

"Yes," I said, and a single tear rolled down my cheek as I looked at the wall, not wanting to acknowledge that it was Angel sitting in front of me.

"Would that make you feel better?" His eyes didn't stray from my face even though I refused to look at him.

"Yes," I said.

"Then get on your hands and knees," he said.

I did as commanded. The tears were falling freely now. Not because of pain or fear. Not because of anger or sadness. No, I was crying in relief. The pressure was going to go away, and I was going to be free of it at least for a little while.

I stared away from Angel at the opposite wall. His clothes rustled as he stripped again. He wasn't going to hurt me and then leave me without his cock. Men didn't know how to watch a woman cum without sticking their cock in her.

"Tell me if it's too much," he said.

A little laugh made its way from my mouth. Too much? He would never be able to hurt me like Marcos had, like my *customers* had.

His hand came down on my ass with a soft smack, and I felt a little sting run through me. The pressure softened just a bit, and I moaned. His hand came down on the other cheek. Soft and gentle. It wouldn't be enough.

"Harder. Please?" I begged softly.

He didn't answer, but his hand came down again, hard enough to leave a red handprint on my ass, and I moaned again, this time much louder. Again and again, his hand came down.

"Harder!" I said urgently. The wall inside me was shaking. I could feel the orgasm waiting inside me. I needed to hurt. I'd been a bad girl, and I hadn't let anyone hurt me in too long.

His hand came down again with the same strength, but this time it landed on my pussy, and the wall shattered. Screaming and writhing on the bed, the orgasm overtook me. Finally, after days of misery, the pressure was released, and I was free of it.

And immediately, Angel was on top of me, his rock-hard cock pressing against my entrance. "Fuck, Maia," he said in my ear. "That was so hot."

His cock filled me just as it had time and time again in the last few days, but this time, I could enjoy it. The pressure began building immediately, as soon as the orgasm ended, but this time, I knew that he'd give me relief.

"Hurt me, please?" I begged breathlessly. Fuck, I needed to cum again already.

His hand went to my hair, and he yanked it hard. His other hand went to my breast and began to twist my nipple. I had hated this before. I had dreamed of the time when no one would use my body like this.

Now, I just wanted Angel to keep doing it. I groaned under him, and he tightened his hold in my hair as he pounded my pussy. The sound of his thighs hitting mine filled the room, and I couldn't imagine feeling better.

The pain that radiated through my breast was nothing. My hair was pulled tight and should have hurt, but it didn't. Only pleasure ran through my body.

I wanted more. Anything he was willing to give, I was willing to take. He released my hair and my breast. His cock slid out of me. What was he doing?

Then he pushed me onto my back. I looked up at him as he pulled me to his cock, sliding me across the bed. He pushed my legs up high, and he ran his cock against my asshole.

He didn't ask, didn't need to ask at all. He looked down at me, waiting for me to object, but I didn't. And he pressed his cock into me. I was ready for him, and he slid into me without any resistance. His hands wrapped around my breasts, squeezing hard as he slowly thrust into my ass.

And the orgasm that had been building rushed through me. He held me down as I lost control of my body, forcing me to take him as I cried out my orgasm. I didn't get to come down from this one.

I'd been forced to take pain my entire life. I'd learned to cum for the men that hurt me. I'd lived with the knowledge that my only pleasure would come with my pain.

This didn't hurt though. Sure, I'd be sore when we were done. His cock was huge, and he stretched me every time he filled a hole, but there was no pain right now. I looked up at him as he pistoned in and out of me, and I saw his true pleasure now. He'd wanted to do this to be before. He'd never asked to use my body like this. He'd never even brought it up.

But he was not a soft man, and he didn't fuck like a soft man.

He bent down and kissed me on the lips, and I kissed back. We were both hungry for more. We were both wanting more than we'd had. When he bit my lip, I moaned for him. This was right. This rawness to him, it wasn't about hurting me. It was about doing what he wanted without a regard for me. It was about knowing that I would feel good regardless of what he did.

That was the difference between him and other men. And that difference felt so fucking good.

He started thrusting faster, harder, rougher, and I felt that familiar burn. It made me want to melt under him. His hands left my breasts and wrapped around my throat. I ran my hands over his arms, softly caressing them as he choked me, cutting off the air to my body.

And he moaned in satisfaction as he filled me. It felt so good to see his satisfaction in his eyes. I smiled up at him as he slowed his motions and rolled over to lay next to me, looking up at the ceiling.

I grinned and rolled off the bed to go clean up. "That was incredible," he said loudly enough for me to hear in the bathroom. He was right. I didn't know that sex could feel like that. My body was a little sore, but it felt alive.

It was like after eight years of a miserable nightmare, I was finally awake. Life was crazy, and things were still confusing, but I was awake. I could fight the things that tried to hurt me now. I could find something worth smiling for. The nightmare was over.

I walked back into the room, and Angel was still laying on the bed, naked. "Are you okay?" he said as he watched me walk trying to determine if he'd hurt me too much.

"I'm amazing. That was exactly what I needed," I said with the widest smile I'd given him so far. I crawled onto the bed and curled up on his shoulder. He was so big. I felt tiny in his arms.

Angel would make a normal girl melt, but I knew that I was putty in his hands as he pulled me close. No one could have convinced me that there was a better man for me. Not now.

"Are you sure? I was pretty rough." I let out a little laugh, and I kissed him.

"That wasn't rough, Angel. That was beautifully sweet sex that I will take any day of the week. Multiple times per day." I looked into his eyes as he took in what I'd said.

"You didn't mind how rough I was?" he asked. I could see the thoughts swirling in his mind.

I gave him a half smile, worried that those thoughts and my answer would change something. "No, I think rough is my normal."

"I guess that makes sense. You've had a pretty messed up life, Maia. I wish I could have found you earlier."

"Me too, Angel. Me too. But I'm just thankful that you found me at all."

He sat up, and I moved so that he could get out of bed. "So... chicken for dinner?" he asked, changing the subject.

"Sure. Chicken. I kind of remember how chicken tastes." I giggled a little. God, it felt good to have that pressure gone. Everything finally felt right in the world.

Chapter 10: Nightmares

Her trail of blood and tears will always
lead them to her. They're drawn to it,
drawn to the pain that fills her body and
her mind like vultures to carrion.

I opened my eyes before Angel today. Four days of glorious exploration of each other's bodies. They were incredible days, and I was living on a high from them. Angel planned to move us to Mexico City tomorrow. He thought that I could do a little exploring of the city if we stayed in certain tourist areas.

The thought of walking around a city was scary, but I trusted him. More than anything, I trusted my savior. He said I needed some time out of a bedroom, and that I wouldn't ever get a chance to see Mexico City again because I could never come back to Mexico after we left.

Sunlight streamed through the curtains, and I stretched out. Angel was still fast asleep, and I looked at him. I was still amazed at how lucky I was that he'd found me and been willing to put himself in danger for me.

He lay on his back with the sheet over his tanned body. I grinned when I saw his hard cock. We'd spent the last week fucking multiple times a day. It wasn't like we had anything else to do. Yet, he was still ready for me.

But this morning, I wanted some quiet, so I didn't wake him up with my mouth. I was satisfied, and I was pretty sure that he was too. I got out of bed and sat in one of the chairs next to the desks. Naked in the warm air, I felt golden. Removed from the real world, with no cares except my hungers, food and sex.

I looked down at the bandage that still covered my brand. It was healing faster than I'd expected and hurt much less than it had. I ran my fingers over the bandage, tracing the letters that would be a part of my skin for the rest of my life.

My consort, a prince among men, lay in the bed. Like a fairytale, I couldn't stop smiling. The motes of dust fluttering through the air were like sparkles from some fairy's wand.

For just that half a second, the world stopped, and I thought of how perfect everything was. Just as quickly, the perfect was gone when I heard the low gravelly voice outside the window.

Angry and Mexican, he was giving orders. Other men responded. This was not the kind of thing that should be happening. I peeked out the window and saw the man. He wore a white button-up shirt and khakis, and he had a pair of sunglasses on. He stood next to a shiny black SUV. There was no mistaking which vehicle they had come from.

Three men were looking at him, and he said something before they walked through the parking lot, looking at the license plates of the vehicles. I let the curtain fall and ran to Angel.

"Wake up, Angel. Hurry up. I think that some of those Cartel guys are here. They're looking at license plates."

He was up instantly. "Get some clothes on. Grab the rest and throw them into your bag." He grabbed his pants and pulled them up. He put on his shirt, but didn't bother to button it. He went to the curtain and looked at the men who were walking through the parking lot. It was still early enough that the sun was barely up. Most of the people in the motel were still asleep.

"Fuck. You're right."

I already had the jeans and shirt on, and I was slipping my shoes on. My heart raced as I began to throw our clothes into the bag we were using as our luggage. Angel had been right to keep the amount of stuff down to a single bag of clothes just in case this happened.

"Get that whiskey bottle," he said, glancing at the bottles of liquor that had come with the room. I turned to look at the bottles and grabbed the one with a golden liquid inside it.

Angel had his knife out of his pocket and had cut a piece of the sheet. With a ripping sound, he tore a long strip off. He looked at the whiskey and smiled. "100 proof. Perfect."

He opened the bottle and liberally poured the whiskey over the strip of cloth. Then he put the cloth into the bottle and twisted the plastic cap back on top of the cloth.

He put his knife back into its sheath and pulled a lighter out of his pocket. "The cartel members are going to be watching our truck. They're probably getting our room information out of the motel clerk already. I'm going to draw their attention away from the truck. I want you to wait until you hear gunshots. Count to twenty, and then you need to run to the truck. Put the keys in the ignition and duck down. Do you understand?"

I nodded, and he smiled before kissing me. Deep and passionate, but urgent. He grinned at me, handed the keys to me, and he said, "Do as I say, and we'll be fine."

"I'll do what you said, Angel. Please be safe. Please don't leave me." I tried to smile, tried to be strong, but I was terrified.

"I'll be fine. Just make sure you do what I said."

I nodded, and he pulled his gun from its holster with his right hand while he held the bottle and lighter in his left. He took a breath and cracked the door open and glanced around before sliding out and closing it behind him.

I peeked through the curtain and watched Angel as he snuck past the black SUV, walking right behind one of the men who was staring at our truck. He positioned himself on the opposite side of the parking lot, the same side as the truck. Seconds passed, and the men came back from the motel office.

The man that had been watching the truck turned to look at them, and they started talking quickly in Spanish and pointing at our room. Almost immediately, Angel began firing, and they took cover behind their SUV.

One... Two... Three... Angel's bullets whizzed through the air, hitting one of the men and making him fall to the ground. The other men began to return fire.

Eight... Nine... Ten... Angel wasn't shooting anymore, but the other men were still popping up trying to hit him.

Fourteen... Fifteen... Sixteen... I was breathing fast, trying to control myself. I moved away from the window, getting ready to go.

Eighteen... Nineteen... Twenty... And I opened the door quickly, sprinting across the parking lot towards the truck. Suddenly, a whooshing sound filled the air, and I glanced back at the SUV which was covered in fire. Several of the men had fire on their clothes, and they were trying their best to put it out.

I opened the truck door and slid the key into the ignition, fumbling with it at first, but managing to get it into the hole. I moved over and got down in the leg space of the truck, panting for breath as screaming and shouting filled the air. Angel got into the truck and started it without saying anything to me.

More screaming as he backed the truck up. Gunshots filled the air. Then we were off, speeding through the parking lot as fast as Angel could go. Without hitting the breaks at all, he turned onto the road and raced off.

"Are you okay?" Angel said intensely without taking his eyes off the road.

"Yes," I squeaked out. "You blew up their car," I said incredulously.

"No, I just put a little fire on it. That won't last though. We have about a minute lead on them, and their car is a hell of a lot faster than ours. We're going to have to get a new car. Something they're not looking for." A small smile crept across his face as he glanced down at me on the floor of the truck.

He made a quick turn onto a side street and then onto another street. He pulled over and said, "Stay down there." The truck idled softly as Angel got out and shut the door.

I finally had a chance to breathe for more than just a few seconds. I couldn't believe how calm he'd been. How had he known just what to do? How had he managed to get us away?

Once again, I was glad that Angel was there. I'd never have been able to keep myself safe if I were alone. Never.

My door opened and Angel looked in at me with a wide smile. He jingled a set of keys in front of me and said, "Grab the bag. I got us a new car."

I crawled into the seat and got the bag with our clothes. Angel already had the passenger door open to the little car. It was tiny. And old. Probably older than me.

I got into the passenger seat and put the bag in the back. The seat of the car was worn out blue vinyl with little rips, and it was hot in the summer heat. Angel closed the door and got back into the truck. With a lurch, he pulled it back into the road and drove halfway down the block before pulling over again. He ran back to the car and got in.

"How'd you get the keys? I thought you were going to steal the car."

He grinned at me. "Nope. Bought it for a thousand dollars. It's a piece of shit, but it runs, and that's all we need. We'll ditch it as soon as we get to Mexico City, but for now, it'll keep the owner from reporting it stolen and telling everyone what kind of car we're driving."

"Oh. That's smart," I said.

"This isn't my first rodeo, Maia. We'll be fine. Today was just a little bump on an otherwise good escape. The closer we get to Veracruz, the better off we'll be. The Sinaloa Cartel doesn't have much sway over that section of Mexico, so other than the whole going to Florida part, we'll probably be pretty safe once we get there.

I leaned my head against the cracked vinyl seat, and I closed my eyes. My pulse was still racing. How was he so calm? How had he known what to do? The questions came back to me.

I'd begun to think about him as my Prince Charming, and maybe he was. Maybe he was the right mix of dark and light for me. But could I handle this lifestyle? Could I be okay knowing that he was risking his life every day and eventually, he'd end up losing it in one of these "bumps"?

No, I didn't think I could handle that. I didn't think that I'd be able to sit at the window every day wondering when he'd come home, wondering whether he'd *ever* come back home.

He would always be my knight in black armor. The man who rode off into the sunset with me, but he'd been right. I shouldn't think of a future with him.

This life that he led wasn't a life that I could handle. I wasn't strong enough for it.

No, I would have to eventually find my own way. I needed to get my mind set on that reality.

Chapter 11: Lost

Tears were her greatest gift. She had not given them to her captors, but she gave them to him. Freely, lovingly, and without any regrets.

You forget how hot the sun is when you live in a cage in the dark. You forget how harshly it will beat down on you as you spend your days in it. Mexico City was an old city, a beautiful city. History was everywhere, and people crowded the streets.

But that sun was brutal. Angel and I sat at an umbrella covered table at a corner café. Angel drank a margarita, but I had a large bottle of water. He was used to the heat, but I was having a hard time.

My long blond hair had been cut short and dyed black. It was hard to get used to, but Angel said it was necessary.

The sandwich lay half uneaten in front of me. My stomach rejected the idea of food. All I wanted was water. "What did you think of the architecture?" he asked.

He was talking about the Mexico City Metropolitan Church that we'd just visited. He'd taken me because he said that Mexico City churches were the most famous in the world, and that I should see them. I didn't understand the draw to churches when I'd spent my life in Hell.

"I don't know. Angel, that's not really something I'm interested in. I've only ever known the architecture of my cell."

"But the arches and domes are beautiful. Even though you've never done very much traveling, you have to admit that those are beautiful."

I shrugged my shoulders. "It's a church. Churches should be spending their money on helping people instead of building golden rooms. It's pretty, but it's wasteful."

He sighed and shook his head. The smile didn't leave his face. He wasn't even hot. Here I was, exhausted, desperate to just go back to our motel room and relax, and he was perfectly happy in the summer sun exploring ancient Churches.

"Is there something a little less artsy that we could see?" I asked, knowing that I wasn't going to be able to convince Angel to take me back to the motel.

"Like what?" he asked.

"Is there a zoo?" He raised an eyebrow at me before leaning back and crossing his arms across his chest.

"There's a zoo, but there are zoos in every major city. We could go to a really big one in Florida too. They all have the same animals. Why would you do that when you can see things that are only found in Mexico City?"

I sighed. "Angel, I remember going to a zoo and loving it. It's actually one of the few memories I have from my childhood."

"Oh," he said as he leaned forward again. "Are you sure you don't want to see any more museums or churches?"

I shook my head. "Absolutely sure. I am completely churched and museumed out. I wouldn't mind seeing a tiger or giraffe though."

Angel shrugged. "To each their own, I guess. We can go look at some animals when you're ready."

I took another big sip of water and said, "I'm ready when you are."

The male lion was bigger than I remembered them being. And lazier. Laying out in the shade of a tree in his enclosure, he was passed out. The cubs bit his tail and jumped on him, but he was so asleep that he didn't notice.

The cubs left his tail alone and began to wrestle with each other, and I couldn't help but smile at them. I leaned against the rail, trying to get a better view through the glass that separated the public from the animals.

Angel's hand wrapped around my waist, and I smiled up at him. He was bored. That was okay with me, though. He'd taken me to all sorts of old places all day when it was supposed to be a day for me to do some sight-seeing. If we were going to have to spend the day in the hot sun, at least I could see something that was interesting.

And those lion cubs were so adorable. The hippos had been too. So had the penguins. And Angel had followed me around the zoo patiently. He tried to be interested in all the animals that I stopped and watched for minutes or longer. I'd stayed with the elephants for almost thirty minutes because a baby elephant was taking a bath. He was so excited and happy that I couldn't convince myself to walk away.

The day was drawing to a close, and I was ready. We'd spent the first half of the day seeing things that Angel had wanted to see, and we'd spent the second half of the day at the zoo. Now it was almost six, and I was ready to get back to the motel.

"What do you want to eat for dinner?" Angel asked, just like every night. I sighed. I didn't know. I never knew.

"How about something from the Yucatan?" he asked. It was hard not to laugh. How was I supposed to know if that sounded good?

"Okay. What does that mean?" He grinned.

"It's from a part of Mexico further south. It's more jungle there. They use a lot more fruit and a lot fewer chilis. They cook with unique things like banana leaves and an orange flavoring unlike anything you've ever had. It's good. You'll probably like it."

"That's fine, Angel. I really don't know why you always ask me what I want when you know so much more about food than I do. I could never have told you that I wanted that, but it sounds good."

"Because it's good for you to practice thinking about things like that. You're going to be all on your own soon. You're going to have to decide things, and it's one of the only things you can decide right now."

It was true. Terrifyingly true. In only a few weeks I'd be making all of my own decisions. Including what to eat every single night. The thought was not something I liked to think about.

"Well, I'd like some of your Yucatan food tonight. There, I made a decision," I said with a grin as I pushed the thought of my looming independence away.

He smiled back and said, "Good because we won't find any places with that style of food for a long time. There are only a handful of places in Florida that make it, and nothing between Mexico City and Florida."

"Thank you for today, Angel," I said as our plates were brought to us. I looked at the bizarre dish. Queso relleno was the strangest thing I'd ever heard of. A small cheese had been hollowed out and then stuffed with pork, peppers, capers, olives, and other things. All of it was diced and mixed together.

And all of it smelled delicious. The cheese was soft and almost melted, and I looked to Angel for how to eat it. He took his knife and cut thin slices to reveal the hollowed-out section that had been filled with all of the delicious bits.

"What for?" he asked.

"For..." I rested my fork and knife on the plate and said, "For pushing me to experience something other than a motel room."

"You're welcome. I'm glad you had a good time for at least part of it." He grinned. "Though I don't know what you see in zoos. They're just prisons for animals. Art is less cruel than zoos."

I shrugged my shoulders. "I've been a captive, and if everyone had just watched me, it wouldn't have been too bad. They don't have to make decisions, and they get plenty of food. It could be worse."

Angel took a bite, and I followed suit. The textures were elegant, and the flavors were perfect. Angel knew food. And art. And how to stay safe from Cartels. He knew a lot about a lot.

"Are you excited about anything in particular when we get to Florida?" he asked.

"I don't know. I've thought about it some. I think I'll enjoy good air conditioning more than anything," I said with a wide grin. Angel laughed out loud.

Mexico was known for a lot of good things, but air conditioning was not one of them. "You know, if you wanted, you could move further north. In the northeastern sections of the US, they don't have air conditioners because it almost never gets hot enough to need one."

I stared at him in disbelief. "Not even in July and August?" I asked.

He shook his head. "Nope. Every once in a while, they'll have a terrible heat wave where it gets to about ninety degrees and people will die. They'll all wish they had air conditioners then, but otherwise, it never really gets much hotter than the eighties."

I blinked a few times. "People die because it's in the nineties? It was almost a hundred and ten degrees outside today and we walked through the city all day long."

"Yep. I've never understood it either. Then again, they go through cold snaps that drop down to negative twenty or thirty. So I guess it all depends on which you hate more, the cold or the heat. I'll take the heat any day of the week. I can do anything in this heat. All day long. But if you put me in negative twenty, I just curl up in a ball and can't move. Even with a parka and gloves and everything."

I thought about it for a second. "I can see what you mean. I haven't ever really been very cold. But when they sprayed me with cold water, it was terrible. Way worse than being hot."

He nodded. "I bet it was." I could see how it hurt him to hear about my captivity, but that was the only lens I could see things through. It was all I'd known.

We ate our food, both of us tired from our day of exploring. It had been a great day, but it was still tiring. I looked over at Angel, and I caught him staring at my breasts with a distant look in his eyes.

I pushed my empty plate away from the edge, and that seemed to stir him from his daydream.

"What were you thinking about?" I asked.

It looked like he was hesitant to say what had been on his mind. "You."

"What about me?" I asked with more than a little curiosity.

"Maia, this is one of those times you may not want to push me. I'll tell you, but remember that I'm not a good guy. I told you from the very beginning that you were safe with me, but that doesn't change the kind of man I am, and the kind of thoughts I have."

I nodded and thought for a moment. "Tell me. If there's something you want me to do, more than likely, I'll enjoy it. I know that you like things rougher than some men, but don't forget that I do too."

He took a deep breath and looked me in the eyes. "I was thinking about what I'd do with you if I had actually bought you. If I owned you like Marcos had instead of rescuing you."

That wasn't surprising. Men enjoyed that kind of control. That's why they spent so much money to use slaves. A hole was a hole, but complete surrender was not common even for whores.

"You'd never get to say no to me. And I wouldn't be kind. I'd tie you up and spank you just for my own pleasure. I'd fuck you and wouldn't let you cum until you were begging me for permission. Then sometimes I'd let you cum and other times I wouldn't. I'd be a lot rougher than I have been."

He sighed. "But I know that those are just fantasies. I don't want to treat you like that." He paused for a second to get his thoughts together better. I waited patiently without saying anything. "That's not true. I'd love to. But I told myself that I wouldn't force you to do anything. I told myself that I wasn't going to become just another Marcos."

He looked down at the table, partly in thought and partly in shame for thoughts he believed were wrong, but I didn't turn away. I was afraid of a lot of things, but sex wasn't one of them. Nothing about sex scared me. Not anymore. Not now that Marcos was dead, and I was free of the Cartels.

"You'll never be like Marcos, Angel. You can't be. He took sex from me. I had no choice. I had no options."

"You say we have probably three weeks left until we leave for Florida. Well, if you hadn't rescued me, then Marcos would have abused me for all of those weeks. I don't have any way to repay that debt. No money or favors to give you. Except this."

I grinned. "How about this? I'll sell myself to you for the next three weeks for a simple agreement. At least two good meals per day, safety from the Cartels, and your continued help in escaping Mexico. If you give me those things, then you can do whatever you want. I'll be your willing slave."

He raised an eyebrow at me and leaned back, crossing his arms again. "Why would you want to do that, Maia? You don't have to. I'm already going to do all of those things."

"I know you are. That's why I'm making you the offer. I want to say thank you, and it's the only thing I can give in return for you giving me my life back."

There was no hesitation in my voice, nor was there any in my mind. It didn't matter what he wanted to do to me. It wouldn't be as bad as Marcos.

Angel hesitated. The offer was too sweet to refuse though. We both knew that. "Then I guess it's time we get back to the motel," he said.

And for the first time since we'd been together, he didn't try to hide the evil side of him. I stared into his dark eyes, and I smiled back at him.

Chapter 12: Service

Never would she forget the fires that forged her. They'd shaped her, tempered her body and her mind. They'd given her purpose and need. A sword cannot change its shape, and it will always crave blood.

$\mathcal{T}$he ropes held me down, but they weren't needed. I wouldn't have moved. He'd told me to stay still. Angel's lips moved over my body, kissing my naked skin, softly, sensuously. Until he reached my thigh. That was where his kisses became sharp bites.

They all bruised as he moved slowly from my knee to my pussy. Some even broke the skin. They should have hurt. Pain should have surged through me like lightning. It didn't though. The three fingers that he was pistoning in and out of my pussy took that pain and turned it into pleasure.

I moaned loudly as he forced a fourth finger into me. I was already close to cumming, and he hadn't even taken his pants off. God, that man knew how to work my body, knew how to weave the pain and pleasure together into a bliss that only he and I understood.

He knelt between my spread legs and continued to fuck my pussy with the fingers of his left hand, but he moved his right hand to my breast. I looked him in the eye as he pinched my nipple between his thumb and index finger. He smiled that wicked smile as he pulled and twisted at it.

I bit my lower lip as I tried not to beg. Not yet. He released my nipple and slapped my face. It wasn't going to take much more. He was going to force me to beg. It was still hard for me to admit to Angel just how much the pain that he inflicted turned me on.

He kept doing it though.

"You're a hot little slave, Maia." His voice was full of lust, full of true enjoyment. Not just the desire that all men get when they have a young beautiful woman under them. No, this was the sadistic desire. I'd heard it over and over again as a man tormented my too young body.

And now I was glad to hear it from the man whom I'd given myself to. He would push me harder, make me cum more. There was nothing wrong with that.

He pulled his fingers out of my pussy, and I knew that they were soaking wet. He ran them across my brand gently. "Slave," he said with a smile. "You're my slave now, aren't you?"

"Yes sir," I said as I looked into his eyes. Eyes that were intent on me and nothing else. Eyes that seemed to peer through my body and into my soul.

"That's a good girl. You'd do anything I asked, wouldn't you?" he asked.

I nodded. "Yes sir," already, the training seemed to overwhelm me again. Only one answer.

He stood up and took off his clothes. I watched him reveal his hardened muscles, a body with scars and marks that showed the roughness of his life. My eyes were drawn to his cock, now aching to be inside me.

He lay on top of me, not trying to enter me. "This is nice, isn't it, Maia?" he asked as he brushed a strand of hair away from my face. "You lying here, and me using your body. You're loving it, aren't you?"

I nodded, and he smiled, showing his teeth. It felt like he was a predator smiling at his prey, a wolf smiling at a rabbit. I didn't want to run away though, didn't want to hide. No, I would have run to this man, run to his touch, run to his pain.

He pressed his cock against my opening, and I moaned as he stretched me. Even after four fingers, his cock still managed to stretch me. Even after days of sex, he managed to stretch me. It hurt in all the right ways.

"It's so nice to be able to play with you without worrying about your pleasure, to tease you, to hurt you, to pleasure myself with your body, all without giving a shit about whether you want it this way."

He wasn't talking to me. He just was letting me hear his thoughts. I appreciated that. It was nice to hear the thoughts that ran through his mind without a filter.

"It's even nicer to look down and see you on the verge of orgasm, to see you trying your hardest not to beg for permission to cum. To know that even as I do whatever I want, it's all exactly what you want too. Maybe I'm your addiction instead of the other way around."

He bent his head down to kiss me, and I gave him everything I had. Every bit of sanity, of energy, of need. I gave it all to him in that kiss, and he took me higher. His teeth latched onto my bottom lip and I tasted blood when he let go.

"Please," I said softly as he began to thrust into me.

"Please what, slave?" he asked.

"Please, may I cum?" I said immediately.

"No."

My body was pulsing with need. I'd waited until I was nearly bursting with the need to cum before begging. And now he wasn't letting me. I groaned out loud as he sped up, trying to think of anything except the searing pleasure that coursed through me.

The white hot need that he forced into my body with his cock and his hands and his lips and his voice. I tried to ignore it all. Tried to focus on anything else, just as I had focused on the opposite walls as I'd been fucked by other men.

Except that this time, I wanted it too much. "PLEASE!," I screamed as he slammed into me harder than he had before.

He just smiled at me. I tried to close my legs. I'd rather push him away than to break the one rule he'd given me. He'd hurt me for a punishment for pushing him away, but he'd keep me from orgasming if I came without permission.

The ropes prevented it though. I hadn't thought that I'd need them. I'd thought that I could control myself well enough. I'd been wrong.

I writhed on the bed beneath Angel, and he smiled wickedly as he watched. Anguish has many realities, and I'd thought that I'd lived in it before, with Marcos. No, that had been pain. Pain was simple. This was anguish, and anguish was terrible.

Yet, I would never turn him down if he offered this to me. He'd been right. I was addicted to him.

"Please. Please. Please," I begged. His smile just got wider as he put his hands around my neck. His fingers tightened, and the air stopped flowing inside me. I tried to scream, but nothing came out.

Just as the colors in the room started to fade, he bent down and whispered, "Cum for me, slave." I exploded in the hardest orgasm I'd ever experienced even without air. And I kept cumming. Over and over again.

His hands must have let me breathe again, but I couldn't remember when. My body shook. My eyes lost focus. Pain. Orgasm. Screaming. Moaning. And finally, nothing.

"Maia," the voice whispered as fingers traced my breast. His voice. Satisfied and no longer hungry.

My eyes opened slowly as his fingers lightly danced across my body. He was watching me already. Black hair, tan skin, green eyes. Eyes that laughed and smiled and danced before me even as he lay in bed with a sleepy expression on his face.

His hand moved lower, to touch the brand that no longer needed a bandage. It was still a little sore, but it needed air. It was strange seeing him trace the letters that my old owner had burned into me. Yet it seemed right. He was the reason that the letters were a trophy instead of a prison sentence.

"Are you okay, Maia?" he asked, and I stretched. My body was sore, but I was okay.

"I'm tired. That's all. What happened?" I asked.

Angel gave me a soft kiss on the arm before saying, "Well, you came and came and came and... oh that's right, you came some more."

I grinned. "I remember some of that. A little bit. Did you enjoy using me? Was it all that you had hoped for?"

He lay on his back and said, "So much more than I could have hoped for. You're incredible, Maia. So incredible."

I was tired. So tired, and so glad that we didn't have to go anywhere. No, all I had to do was enjoy Angel's use of me for the next few days before we moved further south towards Veracruz. Two more stops on the route there.

"You're pretty amazing, yourself," I said and turned towards Angel.

"Tell me a story, Angel. Anything. Truth or lies. Just tell me a story. I haven't heard a story since I was a little girl."

He chuckled a little. "I'm no good at making up stories, Maia."

"Fine. Tell me a real story."

"Are you sure? My stories don't have happy endings," he said. I ran my finger over a large scar that crossed his shoulder. "No stories have happy endings. Eventually, everyone leaves you. I know that."

"Fine. I'll tell you a story about a man who turned a sweet little boy into a villain." I looked him in the eyes. "That sounds like a fine story."

Chapter 13: Baptism

Vengeance is the only thing that matters.
White hot fire that never cools. An eye
for an eye is not enough. Death for an
eye leaves the world without evil men.

*G*ive me your wallet, old man," a voice said from the shadows. My father was carrying bags with gifts for my sister's birthday party. Already wrapped in shiny pink wrapping paper, with a bow on each. My sister was younger than me. Only seven years old while I was nine.

"What?" my father said, turning to the shadows that held the man who had spoken to him. A young man, maybe twenty, stepped out of the shadows with a knife in his hands.

"I said to give me your damned wallet, old man." The knife shook a little as he held it out towards my father. I remember being glad that my sister wasn't there to see what was happening. She'd have been afraid. I trusted my father to handle anything. I knew that my father was a man, and a man could protect himself.

My mother had died when I was younger. She'd gotten into a car accident when I was only three, not long after my sister was born. It was just us three left living in South Texas.

"Boy, put that knife down," my father said to him as he sat the presents on the ground and stood between the mugger and me. The mugger hadn't done this very many times. You could tell from how much he hesitated.

My father was an accountant. He didn't make a lot of money, but many of his customers were criminals. Gang leaders, drug dealers, and even cartel members. He didn't care what they did. He just provided a service, and even criminals do their taxes. It's how Al Capone was caught after all.

Well, he wasn't afraid of a man with a knife in a dark alley, but maybe he should have been. He stepped forward, standing tall and unafraid, like a man would do to a dog that was growling at him. Just like a dog who was cornered, the mugger lunged forward and stabbed my father.

I remember the look of horror on his face as he felt the blade slip between ribs and hit a lung. It had been done purely by chance. The mugger wouldn't have the knowledge or skill to have done it purposefully, but it happened. My father fell to the ground trying to catch his breath, but he couldn't.

"Shit!" the mugger said under his breath and reached for my father's wallet. My father reached up and grabbed his wrist, obviously trying to get the man to help him, but the mugger was less a man, and more a boy. He was scared, and so he lashed out with the knife and somehow managed to cut deep enough into my father's neck that he began to bleed out.

My father wouldn't have died from the stab wound. That's coming from many years of experience and many stabbings. If I had found a phone and called for help, he'd have been fine in a week or two with no major problems.

That cut to the neck though... That was a different story. I knew it as soon as I saw it. Even at nine years old. I jumped up and ran into the nearest store screaming about needing a phone. I called for help, and ten minutes later, men were loading my father's corpse onto a stretcher.

My father was really just extremely unlucky. That boy hadn't meant to kill him. But he had. And that mattered to a lot of people.

Remember how I'd said that my father did a lot of criminals' taxes? Well, he was a likeable man. Always laughing and smiling. Everyone liked him. Even the criminals.

And that night, when my sister and I were supposed to be sleeping at my aunt's house, some of those men who cared about my father came to her house. I remember the commotion. My aunt wanted them to leave, but she was scared of them too. Everyone was scared of them. People who aren't afraid to hurt people tend to get what they want.

At least until someone stops them. That night, those criminals were out for blood. In their minds, a piece of shit had killed a good man who had been a friend. A man who had never hurt anyone, and a man who had helped them.

And they were going to let the son of that man have vengeance. For people who aren't afraid of death, vengeance tends to be important. And these friends of my father were set on the fact that I needed to be a part of that vengeance.

My aunt begged them to leave me be, to let me grieve like normal boys would grieve, like my father had grieved for my mother. They didn't listen, and a single man came upstairs to the room that my sister and I were sleeping in.

"Angel," he said, kneeling down to where he was the same height as I was. His name was Francisco Davila. He'd come to our home and eaten at our table before, but I hadn't known who or what he was.

"We caught the man who killed your father, and we're going to punish him because the police won't hurt him enough. We know how to make him pay for how bad he hurt you."

He put his hand on my shoulder and continued, "You don't have to come with us to punish this man. It will happen regardless, but it's only right for us to allow you to seek retribution."

I looked at him, and I said, "Do you promise that he'll pay for what he did to my father?"

He nodded. "Then I want to come. I want to see him hurt." My words were as confident as a nine-year-old boy could muster. I wanted to see the man punished. More than anything. I was so angry at him.

And so Francisco brought me to a warehouse where the man was hanging from the ceiling with only his toes touching the ground. They'd taken his shirt off, but he hadn't been hurt.

He hung there, tears running down his face. When they told me the story of how they found him after I'd grown up quite a bit, they mentioned that he'd begged and begged. That it had all been an accident.

He'd been right, but the men who had caught him had been thirsty for blood. They were hurting, and they needed to hurt someone. More than anything, they thought that I needed to hurt someone, and maybe I did.

"Boy, this is the man who killed your dad, isn't it?" Francisco asked, and I nodded to him.

He unsnapped a belt sheath he wore and drew out a fourteen-inch hunting knife. Serrated on one side and a razor edge on the other. He flipped it over in his hand and handed it to me, handle first.

I took the knife in my hand and looked up at Francisco. The rage, the sadness, and the fear that had all been boiling inside me had an outlet now. All it would cost to be free of them was my innocence. All it would take was to let the child die and the man replace him.

A thing like this changes you. It's like shedding your skin and suddenly, instead of hands, you have claws. And the claws would always find more flesh to tear into because that is the nature of claws.

I could feel it, that tension as the men around me, the men who already had claws, watched me as I made the decision that would change me forever. "Go ahead, Angel," Francisco said. "Punish him."

I remember the moment clearly. I remember that I didn't smile. I wasn't happy like I would be now. I was nervous, like a boy with his first woman. When I put that razor edge against the man's flesh, he screamed, and I remembered my father.

My father hadn't had the chance to scream. This man had taken even that last sound away from him, and I pulled the knife down across his chest. The flesh split cleanly. Not enough to spray blood everywhere or to be life threatening. Just a little stream of blood down his chest to soak into his pants.

I grew my claws then. The man began to blubber, crying and begging. Nothing like a man should do. I knew that. Even as a nine-year-old, I knew that a man shouldn't act like that. It infuriated me that such a boy had killed my father, and I didn't hesitate.

I pulled back and stabbed upward, just like the man had done to my father. I didn't do it right, and I wasn't lucky. I hit a rib, and it stopped the blade, jarring my strike, and shaking my resolve. It had felt like God himself had flown down and stopped my knife.

The man screamed and writhed and pulled away as best he could. Now I know just how bad that hurt, but at the time, I had no idea what had happened.

Francisco squatted down next to me and held out his hand for the knife which was no longer gleaming silver. Deep red, almost black coated the blade as he took it back.

"Boy, that's not how you stab a man in the chest. You'll hit ribs every time." He grinned at the strung-up man. "Granted, it hurts like a bitch, but that's just going to take some stitches." He turned the knife sideways. "You want to slip it between the ribs. Like this," he said as he walked up to the man and looked him in the eyes.

The knife flashed through the air and pierced his lung, just like he'd done to my father. Francisco handed the knife back to me and said, "You try it." I felt the cold of shock run through me. It had been different when it'd just been drawing blood. I looked at the man and saw that same look in his eyes as I'd seen in my father's.

"Go ahead, boy." I'd watched Francisco, and I knew what to do, but my mind was struggling to make decisions. I was only nine, and this was something that I'd never expected to do.

Francisco had a way about him, though. I felt like I could trust him. Maybe not like a father, but like an uncle. My movements were deft and quick, and I didn't look at the man's face as I pierced his lung. The thing that I remember to this day was the sickening sound that his breathing made. Like a gurgling, bubbling sound.

For years, that sound haunted my dreams. "Good job, Angel," Francisco said and took the knife back. With a quick flick of the wrist, he sliced the man's neck. Blood sprayed as though someone had turned on a water faucet. Francisco and I were both covered in it immediately.

A bloody baptism. Washing away my innocence and replacing it with an awareness of the evil in the world. There was no turning back from that moment. There was no way to shed the claws that I'd grown. Sometimes, I wonder what I would have become had I just stayed home that night.

And that was it. We didn't deal with the body. Didn't watch him as the last bits of life left him. No, once the throat was cut, it was as though the man was dead. Francisco turned me around, and the other men followed us, leaving the man to bleed out.

He brought me to a group of chairs around an ice chest, and he pulled a beer out for each of us. He opened mine for me and handed it to me. "Drink up, boy. Your father's murderer is dead, and you've claimed vengeance. The world is right again."

He watched me as I took a sip. I wanted to spit it out. It tasted like horse piss to my young taste buds, but I didn't. This wasn't the kind of moment that you acted like a child, and men enjoyed beer.

I swallowed the beer, and Francisco nodded. The other men patted me on the back, and suddenly, I was a part of them. They took me in as their own, turned a sheep into a wolf cub, and they were fiercely protective of their cubs.

They taught me how to do everything that they did. Running drugs, pimping whores, and extorting businesses. I knew the basics to everything by the time I was sixteen. Francisco had become almost a father to me by that time. The rest of the crew had become brothers and uncles.

I had a family of wolves, but I'd lost my family of sheep. My aunt and my sister stayed away from me. They didn't want the blood that covered my hands to get on them. They didn't want to be in the world that I lived in. I'm glad that they stayed away, just like I'll be happy for you to stay away from me.

Because, when I was seventeen, a bad thing happened. One of Francisco's sons got on the wrong side of the Sinaloa Cartel, and they decided he needed to die. Francisco wouldn't let that happen, and so he declared war. His crew of fifty versus the empire of the Sinaloa Cartel.

Francisco's entire crew died. Except me. I was on a drug run into Mexico when I heard about it all. He'd known that they would all die, and he didn't want me to die along with them.

He'd neglected to tell me anything, and because I hadn't gotten marked yet because I was still too young according to Francisco, no one knew that I was part of his crew. Suddenly, I was all alone in the world, and there was no way that I could do anything to the Cartel in retribution.

Since that day, almost twenty years ago, I've just continued to survive. That's probably why I decided to take you away from the Cartel. Not because I thought it would punish them for Francisco's death, but because since he died, I don't think I've done anything that could be considered good.

And maybe I needed to do something that wasn't just surviving. Maybe I needed to make a mark on the world beyond just breathing. Maybe you're that mark, Maia.

Chapter 14: Wind

The storm rages without lightning,
without thunder. A dance of wind and
dust and fury. The storm never ends, but
eventually our walk through it will, and
on that day we will rest.

The wind was dry as we walked through Mexico City. Our last day in the most populated city in North America. My last day in Mexico City for the rest of my life because I was never coming back to Mexico. Angel would come back because his business depended on it, but it wasn't known who had taken me.

The streets were dusty today. I was still struggling with the summer heat, but it was getting easier. Angel wasn't pushing me as hard to explore so much. I guess that he'd begun to understand that my body just wasn't used to all the movement. I'd spent my life in a cage, not wandering the streets like him.

"What do you think of this?" I asked him as I held up a bright orange and yellow dress. We'd moved away from the tourist areas and into the local shopping districts. Angel said that I needed clothes that looked

Mexican, not like a tourist trying to pretend to be Mexican.

"That's pretty," he said as he pressed it against my body. The neckline was low, and the bottom would ride higher on my thighs than most of the dresses. He liked it when I showed off for him. We were going to be hiding together on a farm anyway, so I didn't have to worry about people seeing me if I didn't want them to.

I added the dress to the pile that he was carrying for me. "That should be enough, don't you think?" I asked him.

He nodded. "Probably. You probably won't wear clothes most of the time anyway," he said with a wink. The thought sounded amazing. Being free of a cage for the past few days had been great, but I was tired. I needed some calm, and I needed some quiet.

The crowds were overwhelming in the city. Their noise, their motion, their smells, and their jostling were like a weight that constantly pressed on me as I tried to ignore them. I'd never been around this many people in my entire life, and my mind struggled to just let go. I'd been taught to focus on whoever was around me, to see every motion and hear every sound they made. Otherwise, I'd miss something, and I'd be punished.

Now, it was all different, and I was being forced to ignore it all. Somehow, Angel was able to make out important things yet ignore the vast majority of it. That filtering of the thousands upon thousands of people that we passed was incredible and a gift I desperately wished for.

Angel carried the clothes to an old Mexican man standing with an equally old woman. Wrinkled with gray hair, they smiled widely at Angel. Speaking Spanish, Angel talked with them, laughing and smiling. They seemed nice enough, but anyone other than Angel made me nervous.

Angel didn't seem to worry about them, and I'd learned to trust him, so I took a few deep breaths even as the man made multiple sideways glances at me, capturing my image in his mind. Angel handed them some money, and they put the clothes into a bag for him.

He turned away from them and took my hand in his before leading me off to a quieter area of the market where food vendors had set up. We sat down at a table under a canopy, and a waiter came to take our order.

Angel had stopped asking what I wanted, and he just ordered for me. It was better that way. He knew so much more about food. I smiled at him as he handed the menus to the waiter.

"Are you going to be sad to leave Mexico City?" he asked as he sipped on a glass of water.

I shook my head and saw the black hair flash in front of my face. It still surprised me sometimes. "No. I'm ready for some quiet," I replied.

"It will be good to have some quiet before we leave Mexico. It will probably be hard on you once we leave." I nodded.

It was true. I'd accepted that I would struggle in America. I also knew that the human state was a struggle. It wasn't supposed to be miserable, but it wasn't supposed to be easy.

"You'll be fine. You've gone through a lot worse than living on your own, Maia." He had been trying to reassure me for days. I'd been trying to reassure myself. It was still terrifying. I wasn't worried about being caught again. I wasn't afraid of pain and torture.

I was afraid of being too stupid. Of being too unprepared. Of being all alone. What was I supposed to do with myself when there wasn't anyone telling me what to do?

I smiled at Angel, and I told myself the same thing I'd been telling myself the whole time. Everyone manages to take care of themselves. I can do it too. I'll figure it out.

Angel grinned at me, and he said, "Are you sure you don't want to see any more churches?"

I laughed. "I'm sure. I think I've seen more churches than anyone needs to see. I'm probably Catholic just based on how much time I've spent in Catholic churches."

"I just wanted to make sure. It's one of the things that Mexico City is known for." I just shook my head. It had been a running joke since that first day.

And then everything changed. I could see it in Angel's eyes and body language. His muscles tensed, and he looked serious as his eyes traced a man's path. "Look down at the table, Maia," he hissed.

I did as he said, keeping my face covered by my short black hair as I looked down at the table.

"Come on," he said, jumping out of his chair and grabbing my arm. He pulled me along until I was running on my own. "What about the clothes?" I asked.

"Leave them," he said, pulling me into an alley. "They're here. I don't know how they found us, but they did."

"How do you know?" I asked, terror flowing through my body.

"I know him. Antonio Ramirez. Every cartel has a foothold in Mexico City, and he's one of the Sinaloa representatives. The forceful side of it. Maybe he's here just to get a dress for one of his whores, but more than likely, he has men combing the streets for us."

His eyes darted back and forth through the crowds from our shadow in the alley. "See, there's one," he said pointing at a man in dark sunglasses. He walked slowly through the crowd, almost as though he didn't have an end goal. His gaze wasn't on his surroundings or his phone or the road.

He wasn't trying to get anywhere, and he wasn't a tourist, yet he was walking through crowds. That wasn't normal. His face slowly turned back and forth as the crowd surged past his slow pace. He was looking for someone. The dark sunglasses covered his eyes, but it was easy enough to know what his eyes were doing.

"Shit," Angel said. "Antonio isn't an idiot like those guys at the motel were. If he's here, then there's a good chance that they know what our car looks like, and that means that they probably know where our motel is. We need to leave right now. We need to get to Veracruz." He sighed.

"But first, we have to get into a neighborhood somewhere." He thought for a minute. "Stay here, Maia." He pointed at a dumpster and said, "Hide behind that until I get back."

I scrambled behind the dumpster, hoping that no one would come for me while Angel was gone. How had they found us? We'd been careful. Angel had been sure that we would stay under the radar even if we wandered the city.

My body was shaking as I huddled in the shadows, my back against the stone wall. The smell of trash clogged the air, and for a moment, I was brought back to the cell I'd lived in for eight years.

The darkness. The solitude. The fear. The smells and feels and uncertainty filled my mind with memories that I'd tried to forget.

That only made me more uncertain. Angel had to come back. He had to show me what to do.

And then he was back with a new set of clothing for both of us. He tossed me a pair of jeans, a plain blue T-shirt, and a baseball cap. "Put them on," he said sharply. I stripped off my clothes in the filthy alley and put on the clothes that didn't quite fit.

"You're going to have to ride a bike," he said as he put on a cowboy hat, a pair of jeans and a tucked in button-up shirt. "What?" I asked.

"I bought a rickshaw from a boy, and you're going to pull me in it. No one will notice that you're a girl if you're pulling that cart and keep your head down. People don't pay attention to the people working."

My legs already hurt thinking about it, but he was probably right. I followed him out of the alley, and he said, "Follow this street until I tell you otherwise. It's a lot harder for us to hide if we leave the main streets." I nodded, still shaking with fear as I got into the bicycle seat.

I started to pedal and realized that this was not going to be as easy as it had been when I'd been a little girl riding a bike all day. I had to pull Angel and the cart behind me, and there were so many other rickshaws on the street. I just had to do the best I could.

Block by block, I pedaled down the street, and block by block, my legs became more and more exhausted. If there was one thing I knew, it was how to keep going even after my mind told me to stop. One more block. Then another. Then another.

My legs burned. My lungs burned. My vision had become black and white as I continued to push on. I just kept telling myself that it was one more block. Just one more. Then Angel tapped me on the shoulder and said, "Turn right."

I turned the cart slowly, trying hard not to flip it. I kept pedaling. I didn't watch the crowd, and I didn't try to pay attention to the roads to know where we were going. I just waited for the tap on the shoulder, and no matter what else, I kept pedaling.

Minutes went by like hours. My heartbeat pounded in my head and the rest of my body. Finally, Angel said, "Stop here." I hit the brakes, and I sat there, breathing so hard that I wasn't sure that I was going to be able to ever catch my breath.

Angel stood up as colors began to return to my vision. "Come on, Maia. We have to keep going." I didn't respond, couldn't respond. I just got off the bike on shaky legs and looked around. We weren't in the tourist area anymore. Apartments rose up on either side of us.

His hand clasped mine, and he began to jog. My legs screamed at me as I tried to follow him, but I just couldn't keep going. After only a few seconds of running, my leg cramped, and I fell to the ground.

"Maia, we have to keep going," he said in an urgent whisper. I panted on the ground, but I couldn't force my body to its feet.

I felt his hands scoop me up, and he pulled me to his chest. "Hang on," he said as he began to jog down the street. I wrapped my hands around his neck. He loped onward, keeping a steady pace as he wove a path into more and more populated areas.

By the time that he stopped, he was panting softly. I had caught my breath by then, but when he sat me down, my legs still threatened to buckle. I had never worked my muscles to exhaustion before, and it showed.

He looked at me with an appraising eye before saying, "Follow me, but stay behind me when we knock on the door. Don't look at the person who opens the door."

He opened the gate on a chain link fence and walked up to the front door of the house. A stucco one story house with almost no yard. It did have a small garage and a small car in the driveway.

When Angel knocked on the door, I hid behind him with my head down. It was a position I knew well. The man was elderly, probably in his sixties or seventies and had a pot belly, probably from drinking too much beer and eating too many tortillas.

He and Angel exchanged small talk, and then Angel pulled out his wallet. He pointed at the car, and the man's eyes got big. More words in Spanish. Then the man got excited and shook Angel's hand excitedly.

I kept staring down at the ground. Angel didn't want anyone to see my face well enough to remember me.

Angel pulled out many bills from his wallet, and the man moved quickly into the house. He came back only seconds later with a set of keys in his hand. He handed them to Angel, and Angel handed the bills to the man. Then Angel shook his head with a smile.

He held up keys that weren't to the car and grinned at him. The man rubbed his face in embarrassment but accepted the other keys from Angel. He'd handed Angel his house keys along with the car keys. Angel nodded and turned back towards the car.

That's when I saw them. I hadn't looked at the man's face. No, I had been staring at the ground the entire time, but when Angel had moved, I saw the man's boots. Black leather that went up to his calf. An emblazoned silver star on the side.

I began to shake and breathe faster. Angel hurried me into the car before getting into the driver's side.

"What's going on Maia?" he asked seeing the fear and panic that filled my body and mind.

"He was one of Marcos's men," I said in a whisper.

"No, Maia. He was just an old man. We're in the middle of Mexico City. Why would you think he was one of Marcos's men?"

"His boots. They were the same as Marcos's. The same as all of Marcos's men's boots. I'll never forget those boots. Never."

He reached out an arm and touched my face. "Maia, it's okay. Maybe he was part of the Cartel, but even if he was, he doesn't know where we're going. We're fine. I promise."

I looked at Angel. I trusted Angel. He knew what he was doing. "Okay," I said, trying to calm my body down. "Okay, we'll be fine," I said more to myself than to Angel.

Angel nodded and said, "By the time anyone thinks to look outside of Mexico City, we'll be in the safe house, and the car will be in pieces."

I took a deep breath and tried to calm down. He was right. He'd been right every other time. He was right this time too.

Time passed, and I put the incident out of my mind, letting my mind wander towards less stressful things.

We were already headed out of the city, and for a moment, I was frustrated that I was back to having only a single outfit. I looked down at the unflattering boy clothes that Angel had bought for me, and I laughed.

Angel gave me an odd look. "What's so funny?" he asked.

"You're stuck with me dressing like a boy for the next three weeks," I said with a wide grin. "Are you still going to get hard looking at me in boy's clothes?" I asked.

"I'd get hard looking at you in a trash bag, but if there's any issues, I'll just take your clothes away." He glanced at me with a sparkle in his eyes. He was just as ready for time away from the city and the crowds.

Chapter 15: Training

Memories are made in moments. Bright and shining, glorious moments of excitement. Love is made during all the time in between.

Green and vibrant, the land was beautiful. More beautiful than anything I'd seen in recent memory. We weren't quite in Veracruz, but we were close enough. You could even smell the salt in the air from the farmhouse.

I stepped out of the car, and onto the gravel drive in awe. "Welcome home, Maia. For the next three weeks, we'll be living here. Groceries will be delivered. We won't leave for any reasons. It'll just be me and you."

Angel walked around the car to stand in front of me, and he bent down to kiss me. His lips were a drug I could never get my fill of, and I drank of them as long as he'd let me.

When he pulled away, I smiled at him, but that smile turned to surprise as he literally swept me off my feet and pulled me to his chest. Just like he'd done when I was too tired to run. This time, there wasn't any reason for it.

Except when he opened the door to the farmhouse and carried me through it. "We may not be married, but this will be our home for three weeks, and it's bad luck for a woman to walk through the threshold the first time in her home."

I pulled myself up to him and kissed him on the cheek. "It's going to be fun," I said with a gleam in my eyes as he stood me up.

"There's a hundred acres surrounding us, so no one will hear you screaming," he said in a whisper as he bent down to kiss me. I melted into the kiss, enjoying the embrace of his lips against mine.

He released me and said, "I'm going to take full advantage of my little slave." I felt a shiver run through me as the images of how he'd already taken advantage of my body ran through my mind.

"Oh yeah?" I asked a little breathless. I was already getting wet, and my heart was beginning to pound with excitement.

He ran his hands under my shirt and up to my breasts. He still hadn't bought me a bra. "Yeah." He squeezed my breasts in his hands and said, "I'm going to spend the next three weeks doing my best to satisfy my every fantasy with your body."

I squinted my eyes, "What kind of fantasies does a man like you have?"

He bent down and whispered in my ear, "The kind where you cum so many times that you beg me to stop. The kind where you forget your own name." Then he bit my neck hard enough to bruise, and I moaned.

"What do you want me to do then, *Master*," I said with added emphasis on the Master part.

"I like that," he said. "The Master part. It's sexy." He released my breasts and pulled my shirt over my head.

"I'll call you whatever you'd like, Master." A moan escaped my lips as he began to kiss the top of my breasts as his thumb slid under the waistband of my shorts before pulling them down to fall to the floor.

"Oh Master, that feels so good," I said as I ran a hand through his hair. He ran a hand between my legs, and I spread for him. His middle finger found my slit, and I knew he felt the wetness that was already waiting for him.

"You dirty little slave. You already want me to fuck you, don't you?" he asked as he pulled his head up to look me in the eyes.

"Yes," I breathed, and he grinned at me. "Good. Let's get you upstairs so that we can start working on some of my fantasies."

I turned towards the stairs to walk up them, and Angel said, "Wait, Maia."

I turned back around to face him, and I saw trouble in his eyes. "Are you sure about this?" he asked.

"About what?" I responded.

"This whole you being my slave thing. You don't have to do it. You know that, right?"

"Will you enjoy it?"

He hesitated, but he responded, "Yes."

"Then do whatever you want with me. If I tell you to stop, please stop because it means that something is really wrong, like I need a doctor kind of wrong, but otherwise, just do whatever you want with me."

On one hand, I was trying to give Angel something as a thank you, but after having fucked him for the past week, I knew that I'd enjoy it too. It wasn't the same as it would have been with Marcos. This wasn't just a gift to Angel like I'd meant it originally.

"Okay, then go up the stairs and to your right. Bend over the bed. I've been wanting to spank that ass of yours since I saw you naked the first time."

My legs wouldn't move fast enough as I ran up the stairs and bent over the bed. We'd been in the car for hours, and my body wanted him. The way his eyes got hungry when I was being submissive, and the way his hands crawled over my body like he owned me. I heard him pull his belt loose from his pants as I climbed the stairs.

I'd felt the sting of a belt on my ass plenty of times in my life, and I had hated it every time. I was sure that this would be pure bliss and ecstasy though. I had fantasized about a time where I wouldn't have sex anymore. Now, I couldn't imagine a life without sex.

It was different when you chose it. It was different when you wanted a man's hunger directed towards you. I turned to looked at the door to the room and saw Angel holding the belt doubled up in his hand. His shirt was off and laying on the floor. Hard abs and a strong chest showed his physical strength, but the interlaced scars that lay across his tan skin showed the strength that mattered.

That was a man who had faced death over and over again, and he'd won. Scars were just symbols for the times that you'd won because in the life that Angel lived in, you either won or you died. Those scars had taught him how to become the man who could steal from one of the most dangerous criminal organizations in the world and get away with it.

That man and the strength that he wielded was a firebrand, lighting my body on fire with desperate lust. He smiled at me as he unbuttoned his jeans and let them drop to the floor along with his boxers, leaving him naked.

A shiver ran through me as he approached. His hand went between my legs, spreading them. His finger pressed against my entrance, and my body accepted it without a bit of hesitancy. I was ready for him. Desperate for him. A soft smile crossed my lips as he pushed his finger to the back of me.

"You're soaking wet, slave," he said.

"I know, Master. Wet for you." He pulled his finger out of me and put his left hand on the small of my back. "You're not allowed to cum unless I allow it, slave. Do you understand?"

Those were terrible words. I'd told him that he could do anything he wanted with me, but those were more difficult and painful to accept than any kind of sex or beating.

"Yes sir," I said.

Then the belt swung. He hit my ass hard, but I didn't cry out. It stung, but pain was a strange creature. Sometimes it was unbearably unpleasant, but right then, I melted into it.

Red lightning raced through me as the belt came down again. I moaned and relaxed onto the bed. I knew that my ass was red with welts beginning to rise from my pale skin. I knew that if he kept hitting me that hard, I'd be bruised soon. I didn't care about either of those things.

I cared about the growing need inside of me. I cared about the fact that my body wasn't allowed release. More than anything, I cared about him taking too long between strikes.

Again he swung, crisscrossing the first strike. This one came down and clipped the bottom of my butt cheek, and I stuck my ass out further.

On the fifth one, I heard the belt fall to the ground. Part of me squirmed in fear, but the other squirmed in excitement. He could be done with me, but he might also be getting ready to do something more.

I tried to breathe deeply, to calm my body, but it wasn't working. His hand wound itself into my hair, and I moaned as he balled his fist. Then I felt his cock at my entrance, and I pressed backward, desperate for him to fill me up.

He wasn't easy about it. Not this time. He rubbed himself against my entrance, slicking himself up on my juices before slamming into me. I'd been moaning before, but that silenced me. It was all I could do to keep myself from begging him already.

He bent down, pressing his hard chest against my back, and he whispered in my ear, "Are you ready to beg, slave?"

I shook my head. This was the game he wanted. He wanted me to hold back. He wanted to rip that orgasm from my unwilling body. He didn't want to control me with pain. No, that would have made him the same as all the other men. Instead, he controlled me with orgasms.

He knew how to play my body. "You will," he whispered. He thrust in and out of me a few times, but then he pulled out of me. A groan escaped me without my knowledge, but it was quickly replaced with whimpering.

He pressed against my asshole, and I didn't try to keep him out. I wouldn't have won that battle. It hurt. There was no way that a cock that big would be able to enter my ass without it hurting a little.

And I loved it. He'd been right. As his balls pressed against my pussy lips, I began to beg.

"Please let me cum," I said in a whine.

"No," he said as he forced my face into the blanket. His cock slowly pulled out until only the tip was still inside of me, and then he rammed it back in. He knew I could take it. I knew I could take it.

But could I keep from cumming?

I struggled to breathe through the blanket, and I tried to get away from his grasp, but it was an unbreakable grasp. Seconds ticked by as he did the same thing again, and I groaned into the bed.

Then he let my head up, and instead of trying to get a breath, I begged more, "Please let me cum. Please. Please. Please."

Immediately, he forced my head back into the blanket. His cock sped up. He slapped my ass with his other hand, and I could feel my pussy juice running down my leg.

I needed to cum so badly. There was no wall to keep it bottled up, and only through strength of will was I keeping it back. And that strength was failing.

"If you cum, I'll have to punish you, slave. I'll take away the pain and let that need build and build and build for days."

I felt tears begin to well up, not from the pain, but instead from the effort of keeping my body from letting go. I remembered times before. Times in the dark of a cell where a nameless man used my body. I remembered times where I didn't think I could handle the pain, where I would die if the pain continued.

They didn't compare to this. I could give up and give in then, but now, I had to stay in the moment, feeling every stroke of his cock, and not let my body do what it had been trained to do.

Angel let go of my hair, and I lifted my head up, hoping that being able to breathe would give me a little bit more control over my body. It didn't. I moaned and groaned as he pounded me. I was building my own wall, stone by stone inside of myself.

Finally, Angel stopped pounding my ass and leaned over me. His hands reached under me and gripped my breasts as he whispered in my ear. His fingers pinched my nipples as he said, "Do you want to cum, slave?"

I instantly responded, "Yes. Please. Please. Please." His fingers squeezed my nipples harder, making the need inside of me ever more persistent.

"If you cum, you're not going to be allowed to stop cumming until I cum. Do you understand, slave?"

"Anything you say, Master," I responded. I could almost hear the evil grin that crossed his face. He pulled out of my ass and laid down on the bed next me.

"Then fuck your ass with my cock," he said. He didn't have to say it twice. I could ride a man for hours. I'd done it before.

I crawled onto the bed and straddled him, my body facing him. His cock was so hard. He wanted this just as much as I did.

I slid down on top of him, feeling him fill me up. Most of my juices had dried up, and it hurt, but that only made it easier to cum.

Up. Down. Up. Down.

And then the wall I'd started to build exploded with a scream. Angel just lay there and watched me as I came. My body didn't stop pistoning up and down. I started breathing more normally, as the orgasm passed through me, and I smiled softly.

"Don't you dare stop cumming, slave. That was the deal." His voice was hard, and I remembered that there was more darkness than light inside the man that I'd given myself to.

He gripped my breasts tightly and slammed upward into me. My ass tightened around him, and I let go. Pain wove its way through my body, and I released it in a loud moan.

I was nothing but a toy that turned pain into pleasure for Angel. I had said that I'd give myself to him to use, but that had been words. This was the moment when that deal was made real. It was sealed in pain and stamped with screams.

He let go of my breasts, and one hand wrapped around my throat. The other slapped my face with a loud crack. Not hard enough to leave a bruise, but more than enough to leave a handprint across my cheek.

Up and down. Up and down. My body tightened as the orgasm raced through me again. The hand around my throat tightened, and I felt the air to my body stop once again.

Up and down. Up and down. He was getting impatient. He was slamming his cock into me harder and harder. So close.

Up and down. Up and down. He used my throat as leverage to thrust into me harder. He grunted. The colors began to dim. My lungs burned.

Up and down. Up and down. My body ached as another orgasm forced every muscle in my body to tense. Blackness was creeping into my view. My hands went to his hand.

He grunted and let go of my throat, leaving me gasping. His hands grasped my hips and held me down as he filled my ass with his cum. His expression was serious as he came inside of me.

Then he was finished, both of us breathless as I sat on him, staring at him as his expression changed. Just moments ago, he'd been tempted to choke me into unconsciousness. He would have continued to use my ass until I woke up.

Now, he was turning back into the man who had laughed as I'd watched lion cubs with glee. The man under me now was the one who couldn't wait to show me a new food or tell me about things he'd done in his travels.

There was a part of him that was darker than anyone I'd ever met. A part of him that could watch a man die without any sympathy. A part of him that had tortured men and women without any problem.

There was another side of that coin though. He'd enjoyed showing me all of the things in Mexico City. He'd risked his life for mine, and he wasn't keeping me. He was giving me the freedom that I'd dreamt of.

No one would say he was a good man, but he was good to me. More than that, he understood me and understood the broken inside of me.

I rolled off of him and went to the bathroom, finally taking things in now that my pussy wasn't controlling my mind anymore.

As I recovered, I looked around for the first time. The house was wooden with white paint in all the rooms. It flecked in places, but more from disuse than from misuse.

Dark stained wooden floors had been cleaned recently. If no one lived here, then someone must have come in and cleaned the place or there would have been inches of dust and dirt.

I cleaned up and walked back into the bedroom to see Angel still laying naked in the bed. The bed was still made, though our activities had rumpled it some. The comforter was a pretty flower design. Angel smiled at me.

"You're beautiful, Maia." I stood in front of him, and I didn't bother to cover up as his eyes roamed over my body, a hint of hunger still there. That look stirred desire that had just started to sleep again.

"Now, I thought I was going to be your slave while we were. Slave, not Maia." I put my hands on my hips, feigning seriousness.

He put his feet on the ground and stood up, towering over me before he bent down and gave me a kiss that took my breath, and my seriousness, away. One hand went to the back of my head, and the other went to my waist as he pulled me into the kiss.

That stirring became more insistent. When he pulled away, he left me breathless.

"Absolutely not!" he said seriously as I tried to catch my breath. "I don't want a slave. I want a beautiful woman who will do anything I say. I want to own your body sexually, but I want you to laugh and play and be you. I may torture you in the bedroom, but I don't want you to be anything other than Maia when I'm done pleasing myself with your body."

He put his hand under my chin and lifted my gaze up to meet his even as I naturally looked down at the floor. "Do you understand?"

I nodded. "Yes sir."

"Good. Let me show you the house now that I'm not starving for your body anymore."

He put on his clothes again, and said, "You'll need some clothes for this." I nodded and put mine back on.

The house was simple. Plain, but well cared for. There had been no neglect even though there were defects in places. The floors had scuff marks, and the walls had chips in the paint throughout the house.

Yet there was no dust. The furniture wobbled a little bit, but there were no cobwebs. The kitchen was clean even though it seemed like the appliances were old.

"Is this your house?" I asked Angel as he finished the tour.

"Kind of. I have a deal with the owner, George. I can come by any time I want, and I pay a significant amount of money to do so. George and his wife make sure that the only people that come by are them. He'll be buying our groceries, and you may see him taking care of the stables and the pool. Other than that, he won't bother us."

"Stables? A pool?" I asked with a wide smile.

"He has a few horses which we're allowed to ride if we want to, and there's a pool which is the main reason that we're staying here."

"Show me!" I said, barely keeping the squeal out of my voice. I'd always wanted to ride a horse. Now I was going to get to spend three weeks riding horses and swimming? This couldn't be any more perfect.

Angel grinned. "I thought you might like the stables, but let me show you the pool first. There are some things I need to talk to you about."

He was being serious again, and I had to remind myself that he was a serious man. He had to be serious, and I had to accept that, but that didn't change my desperate desire to see the horses.

He led me out to the Olympic sized swimming pool. It wasn't meant for children. It was long and thin, and it was obvious that it was meant for swimming laps. Just like the rest of the house, it was well maintained with crystal clear water, but paint was chipped and faded.

"Do you know how to swim, Maia?" he asked.

"I could swim when I was little, but it's been a long time," I said, itching to get into the water.

"Good. Your only job while we're here is to become the best swimmer you can be. Part of how we're going to get to the states involves you swimming for about half a mile through the ocean. That means that you need to be able to swim a mile by the time we leave. That's just about thirty-two lengths without stopping."

That was a long swim. A very very long swim. I could swim a lap or two when I was a little girl without a problem, but thirty-two? I hadn't done anything like that before.

"What happens if I can't?" I asked Angel.

"Then I'll have to try to pull you the rest of the way, but I don't know how far I can manage to drag you. You can get strong enough to swim that far. You don't have to do it fast. You just have to be able to do it without stopping."

I took a deep breath. I could do that. That's all I had to do. Just swim. No other responsibilities. Just swim.

"Okay. I'll do it." Angel gave me a smile and said, "Now let's go see those horses."

I grinned and bounced as I followed behind him. I'd seen horses. Everyone had seen horses, but these were basically ours while we were here. As we walked from the house to the barn, I looked around and was amazed at how isolated we were.

There was no one within sight. No houses, no road, nothing except us, the house, and the barn. The stables were attached to the barn. Two horses poked their heads out of the shaded enclosures. They seemed interested in us as Angel opened a squeaky gate that surrounded the area around the barn.

"Can I touch them?" I asked Angel as we got close.

"Move slowly, and stay on their side," he said as he led me to the larger of the two, a gray colored horse. He patted the horse's neck, and I did the same. The horse brushed its head against mine, not hard enough to hurt, but enough that I couldn't ignore it.

I giggled as I patted and pet its neck. "That's a good horse," I said softly as I looked into his eye. Angel stood behind me, watching.

"Remember to always make sure that the horse knows where you are, and don't stand behind them. Scared horses can hurt you, and the way they hurt you easiest is by kicking you."

I nodded. "Stay on their sides, not in front of them, and move slowly but surely."

I turned to Angel and hugged him. "Thank you, Angel. Thank you so much." I'd been ecstatic to be free of Marcos. I'd been excited to see the world. But I'd dreamt of riding horses since before I could remember.

Once again, Angel was turning a dream into a reality.

Chapter 16: Floating

In the silence she found the spark, and in the darkness she fed it. He had given her kindling, but only she could care for this flame.

The water was cool when I stepped into the pool for the first time. I didn't wear a swimsuit. I didn't have to wear clothes for swimming, and so I didn't. It made me feel more comfortable, more natural.

Angel was cooking steaks in the house, and I hadn't known what else to do. I only had one real job: become the best swimmer I could be. I had decided that I might as well start training tonight. The real world disappeared as I dove into the water and let it swallow me up.

Weightless and completely surrounded by the water, I floated in the nothingness. Peace flowed through me in the silence. No one needed me to do anything. I didn't have to think or do or feel anything for anyone. I just needed to exist.

It was a fleeting experience as my breath ran out, and I swam back to the surface, but it was there, and it was real. I didn't know what it meant, but for that moment, I had felt free beneath the surface.

I smiled as I looked back at the house. Angel wouldn't understand. Angel had grown up with freedom. He'd been able to do anything and go anywhere.

This was one of *those* moments for me. One of those times that you can feel something inside of you shift. Yesterday, I'd been a girl who was being rescued by a beautiful man. The damsel in distress. Now... now, I *had been* rescued.

Now, I wasn't waiting on a man to save me. There were still steps, but I was free right now. I wasn't a prisoner, and I wasn't in the middle of an escape. I was free. Lazing about in a pool while a sexy man cooked my dinner. I was free.

Something snapped inside of me. I had given my body to Angel to use as a gift, but I wanted it just as much as he did now. I was free.

But that meant that I couldn't expect someone else to take care of me anymore. I had to grow up. I had to remember that I had a responsibility. I was the only one who could push my body to become strong enough to live through the final piece of the escape.

I smiled as I surfaced. Water streamed off me as the sounds of the world came back to me. I took a deep breath and looked at the end of the pool. That image of a long glassy strip of water stuck in my mind.

No different than any other tunnel, this was the vision I had when thought about the next three weeks.

Naked and staring down a tunnel made of water. Nothing to save me except my own strength. Only I could push myself through the water to the end of this journey.

That was fine with me.

I pushed off the side of the pool and began to swim.

"Maia, the steaks are all done," I heard as I grabbed the edge of the pool and gasped in air. Sixteen laps, each one done separately, but still, sixteen laps was hard work, and I was exhausted.

"Okay, I'm coming," I said as I flipped my hair back. I took a few more deep breaths and pulled myself up the side of the pool.

It was strange to walk around naked outside, but it made sense, and it felt good to be in the pool naked. I had imagined wearing a swimsuit, and the thought made me itch. The stretchy fabric pulled tight against my body sounded miserable. I hadn't worn many clothes when I'd been a slave, so the restricting kinds of clothes still felt very uncomfortable to me.

Angel handed me a towel before bending down to peck my cheek. "Seeing you in the pool like that was hot," he said as he turned back towards the house. I raised an eyebrow towards him, but he didn't see my expression.

"Why?" I asked.

"Because you're training your body which is sexy and because wet women are sexy. Plus, I like the way that your tits look in the water," he said with a smirk.

Was it bad that I could tell that he was smirking even though I couldn't see him? How had I come to know him that well already in just a little over a week?

When we walked into the house, the smell of steaks was overwhelming, and I realized how big of an appetite I'd worked up. "Oh my god, Angel. Those smell incredible," I said.

"I'm glad. I hope you're hungry because you can't get this quality of steaks in little girl portions." He turned to show me the smile that crossed his face.

"You'd better be careful, Mister. I might just steal your steak to prove how much of a big girl I am."

He laughed and shook his head. "If you want my steak, I'll give it to you, Maia. Somehow I doubt that you'd be able to eat two and a half pounds of steak along with grilled asparagus." He pulled a plate from the cabinet down and scooped a massive steak onto the plate. Then he heaped it with asparagus spears that had charred edges from where he'd grilled them.

"Do you think you'll need a second one now?" he asked. I shook my head as I looked in awe at the portion.

"No, I think this will be enough," I said as I carried my plate to the table.

"That's what I thought," he said, following behind me.

He set the plate down and went to the refrigerator. "Would you like a beer?" he asked. I hesitated. I'd never had a beer. I knew that they were supposed to taste bad at first, but I wanted to try it.

"Yeah." He popped the top on both his and mine, and he set them down in front of us. It was a glass bottle with a golden liquid inside of it, bubbles rising to the surface.

I gave him a half-hearted smile before taking a sip of the beer. It tasted terrible. Bitter and sour and bubbly. Why would anyone want to drink beer? I must have made a terrible face as I swallowed it.

He grinned and went to take it from me. I'd asked for it, and I wanted to prove that I could handle drinking something I'd asked for, so I held onto it.

Angel nodded and took a drink of his before cutting into his steak. I took another look at the beer before deciding to cut into my steak first. Red and juicy, it looked wonderful.

I took a bite and let the flavors sit in my mouth as I chewed. Everything about that steak was perfect. It was tender, full of flavor, and still tasted like it'd been cooked over a fire. Almost as amazing as the man who had made it.

Now, I have had a lot of good food since I met Angel. It seems to be one of the things that Angel was passionate about, but I had never had anything that he'd cooked. It was far superior to any restaurant food we'd had so far. Less complex than a lot of it, but far better in flavor, and the simplicity of the meal was nice. I knew what I was eating.

He sat next to me in just a pair of jeans and a plain black T-shirt, and he couldn't have been sexier. "This is the best food I've ever had in my life," I declared. He grinned and shrugged. "I like good food."

I guess it was as simple as that. Once you were in charge of your own food, you had to get good at cooking it, or you'd be stuck eating bad food forever. I would have to start watching him cook so that I could do it when I was on my own.

He looked out the window and took a sip of his beer. "I hope that your first day in paradise has been enjoyable," he said. I looked out the window, trying to see what Angel saw, but I couldn't.

"It's been wonderful," I said.

He nodded. "That's good. I've always enjoyed this house," he said. He had thoughts swimming around in his head, but I couldn't figure them out.

"What's going on, Angel?" I asked.

He turned to me with a smile. "I was just thinking about how these next few weeks are going to fly by, but they're also going to be such a nice change from the busy life I normally lead."

"That makes me a little scared," I said.

"What do you mean?"

"Well, I just don't know how to do stuff. I don't know how to be busy. What if I forget to go to work or something like that?"

He tried to keep himself from laughing too much, but I saw the look in his eyes. He thought I was an idiot for having those fears.

"Maia, you aren't going to forget stuff. You haven't forgotten anything since we've been together. And if you forget, then you deal with it and move on. It's not like someone is going to beat you or kill you for making a mistake."

"I know that, but people fail at a normal life all the time. They spend all their money on stuff, and then they can't pay their rent, or they get their electricity turned off, or they... I don't know. They fail at life. I haven't ever had to do any of that stuff. I don't know how to do any of it, and maybe I'm just too stupid to live in the real world. Maybe I'm only good at sex and letting men hurt me. Maybe I'm too broken to be normal."

He stared at me, no longer trying to keep himself from laughing. Seriousness and hardness raced in his eyes. "You're not too broken for a good life. You're a light in the world, and even after all the years of pain, you haven't lost that spark. I will not let you say those kinds of things again. You're worthy of more happiness than anyone I've met."

He took my hand in his and squeezed it. "I will always be there for you. Even if I'm not at your side, I'm just a phone call away. You'll make mistakes. Everyone does that. You'll forget to pay your bills or forget to buy groceries. Do you know what happens if you forget things like that?"

I shook my head, and he smiled, softening a little. "You have to pay a little extra. That's all. The absolute worst thing that will happen to you is that they'll stop letting you live there, and then I'll give you some money, and you can pay the bills."

"It's not like this world that you've lived in for so long. No one will beat you. No one will kill you. It's all just money and luxuries. Even living on the street and eating out of garbage cans would be better than what you had with Marcos, but I won't let that happen. You're going to be fine. Do you hear me?"

I nodded my head and calmed down a little. He let my hand go as he said, "Good. Now, I did want to talk to you about something. Right now, the only thing that you have to do is to swim. How would you feel about me teaching you some self-defense classes?"

I hesitated for a moment. The thought of fighting a man like Angel, even if it were only for practice, scared me. Then I remembered the moment in the pool today. I needed to grow. I needed to be a person who could live in the world without a protector, without guards and a steel cage to protect me from the world.

"Okay," I said. I probably should have more words. I didn't know what to say though.

"Great. We can start that tomorrow. I won't be there to protect you, but I can't stand the idea of some asshole hurting you because you're alone."

"You're right. I need to be able to keep myself safe." I took a long drink of the beer. After that conversation, it didn't taste quite as bad. I still would never choose to drink this if I had a choice, but now that I knew what it was supposed to taste like, it didn't make me instantly gag.

We ate the rest of our meal quietly, both of our minds filled with thoughts. I had lived within my thoughts for so long, but now it seemed almost strange to sit and stare, letting them run their meandering courses. It was hard to keep my distance from the man sitting next to me.

He was so protective, so solid in his strength. Yet, I knew that if I stayed with him, that he would bring nothing but difficulty to my life. He lived in a whirlwind, pulling in trouble and throwing out dead bodies. I hadn't dreamed of that when I'd sat in my cell and fantasized about the normal world. I had dreamed of horses and houses, good food and good friends. Not bodies and fear. And though Angel offered the former, you couldn't separate the latter.

I would have to find my fantasy on my own in the real world. No matter how tempting it was to take the easy way out and tie myself to Angel, my happiness would only be found on my own.

Chapter 17: Flying

A broken bowl can be pieced back together, but there will always be missing chips. The bowl will never hold water until the missing pieces are replaced with something new.

H ow do we ride horses?" I asked. A simple question that any child who had yearned to climb on the back of the beautiful animals and ride with the wind should have had the answer to. I didn't know, and I'd hazard a guess that most children didn't either.

"I'll show you. It's not that tricky with well-trained horses like these, but with some of the wilder ones, there's a lot more to it." The gray horse stood in the stall with Angel, looking majestic and kind, and Angel began to put all of the riding gear on.

"How do you know so much about so much?"

"What do you mean?" he gave me a quizzical look as he put the saddle on the horse's back.

"Well, like how do you know how to ride a horse? Do you have horses?" I leaned on the gate as I stood outside the stall and looked in.

"No, I don't have any horses. Though I've thought about it. I had to take a horse through Columbia at one time because there had been a blockade set up to catch me. I bought a horse, much like we bought the cars, and I had the old Columbian who owned it teach me how to ride."

He tightened the straps along the girth of the horse and started on the bridle. "I realized that riding a horse was something that I enjoyed. Just like some people have boats or motorcycles that they take out on the weekend, I occasionally will rent a horse for a weekend and just go riding in the mountains."

"It's freeing to be away from the world and everything that stands for it. No phones, no money, and no cars. Just you and a horse on a trail. Like it used to be before the world got so crazy. It's the way that people are supposed to travel. We've been riding horses for thousands of years, but all of a sudden, we invent cars, so we don't ride them anymore. Our bodies still remember the way it feels to ride a horse. It's natural."

I looked up at the massive animal and shook my head. I couldn't imagine how it would feel to control anything that big. I could barely imagine riding on its back, much less telling it what to do.

"That sounds nice, but they're huge. How do you make it do what you want? I've always wanted to ride a horse, but now that I'm standing next to it, I don't think I'd be able to force it to do anything. I mean, it's just so much bigger and stronger than me."

Angel tightened up a few straps and smiled at me. "You can't make a horse do something you want. You can't stop it from doing what it wants. All you can do is make it harder for it to ignore you. Then you wait until it gets exhausted, and eventually it will do what you tell it to. Most of the time."

"But that's not what's going to happen with these. They're well trained and well ridden. They won't balk at your commands. They may whine a bit, but they'll do it."

"What do you mean my commands? They understand English like when you tell a dog to sit?"

That brought a bit of laughter from Angel. "No, you use the bridle to turn them and you use your legs to make them move at the right speed. Horses are smart, especially ones that are older like these. They can read your body language, but there's not a stop and start button on them. You have to do the right thing, or they'll laugh as they follow your direction into the bushes."

That made me hesitate even more. Could I control them?

"You'll teach me, right?"

"I wouldn't be out here if I wasn't going to teach you, Maia."

"And you won't let them hurt me?"

"I won't let them hurt you. Just listen to what I say, and you'll be fine."

He smiled at me as he turned around. "Now for the brown one."

I watched as Angel galloped across the field, moving faster than I could imagine. Trotting had been tough, but I'd finally gotten it. My thighs hurt, and my hands were sore from holding the reins so tightly, but I felt like I was soaring. I'd wanted to ride a horse my entire life, and here I was.

"You need a name, horse," I said. "I'm sure you already have one, but I don't know it." The horse whinnied in response.

"You sure do whine a lot," I said. Angel was waiting at the stable smiling. He was pushing me to control the horse on my own now, and this was just one more way.

I squeezed my legs together and steered the brown horse towards the stable. He started to walk, but he wasn't in any hurry.

"You don't like moving much either, do you?" I asked the horse as we walked. He gnawed on the bit and shook his head.

I squeezed my legs together again, and he began to trot. I'd gotten the trot down a bit better, but it was still a rough ride. Tomorrow I wanted to try to gallop. Angel had promised that it was a lot smoother of a ride, but I didn't think I was ready for moving that fast. Not today at least.

Even at a trot, the brown horse seemed slow. "Come on," I said to him. He didn't respond to the request, but his trot was eating the distance between us and the stable fast enough that I tried to just hang on. My thighs were going to be aching tomorrow.

There was no amount of exercise that could have trained my body to ride a horse. Yet, just as Angel had said, after only a day of riding, I felt relatively confident in it. It did seem natural even though my body wasn't used to it.

When I got to the stable, I pulled back on the reins and we slowed down and stopped next to Angel. The horse whinnied again, and Angel grinned.

"That horse is a whiner," he said. "And slow. I'm pretty sure that the gray would have beaten him back to the stable at a walk."

I laughed and patted the horse's neck. "I think he's more of a donkey and less of a horse, like Eeyore." I giggled a little at the thought. "That can be your name. Eeyore, like in Winnie the Pooh." Angel just grinned at my conversation with the horse. He didn't seem to talk to his horse very much.

"It's okay, Eeyore," I said as I ran my hand over his neck. "What are you calling your horse, Angel?" I asked him as he climbed off the horse.

"Gray?" he said sounding a little confused.

"That's a terrible name for a horse," I said with full confidence.

"So is Eeyore since Eeyore was a donkey."

"Well, fine. Your horse can be named Gray, and mine is Eeyore. Terrible names for great horses."

"Old horses," he mumbled and gave Gray a wink.

"Come on, let's get you off Eeyore. The old horse needs his nap time, and I need a snack."

Chapter 18: Pleasure

Change is painful. Growth is painful.
Life is painful. Pain is the way that the
world forces you to prove that you deserve
anything, but when pain is pleasure, the
world is left powerless.

I reached my hand under the sheet and felt his cock. Hard and strong and throbbing. I needed him badly enough that my body ached for it, but I would have to earn my relief. It had been two days since I had cum, and he had been serious about me earning my next orgasm. Begging to be spanked hadn't been enough for him. My ass still hurt from last night.

Maybe if I teased him. It had been two weeks at the farmhouse, and Angel had enjoyed the use of my body more than I'd expected. I hadn't believed that any man could fuck three times a day for two weeks, but Angel seemed to exceed my expectations in almost every way.

I took his cock in my hand and slowly crawled down to position myself correctly, careful not to move it too much. He was laying on his back, and his cock stood straight up. Even in the darkness, I knew what to do, how to move my body.

His legs were spread, and I put my arm between them to support myself. My fingers held him lightly, but his body responded almost instantly to the stimulation. He'd been snoring lightly before I'd touched him. Now, the snoring had changed into soft moans.

I would enjoy this control, this freedom to play with his body while he slept. It wouldn't last long, or at least I didn't expect it to. He was too light of a sleeper. I ran the tip of my tongue over the head, and he thrust his hips towards me. He never would have done that if he'd been awake. He'd never have shown me his need.

Now, I could see and feel what he wanted to do but wouldn't allow himself to do. A few drops of precum spilled from the tip, and I licked it up, enjoying the taste before taking the rest of his head into my mouth and gently sucking on it.

My hand began to move up and down the shaft, not quickly or roughly, but enough to make him throb even more. This was about making him feel the same need that I did. I needed him to be desperate.

His body was mine for these few moments, and I needed him to wake up ravenous for me. I needed him to be rough, to have none of the control he typically showed me. I needed him to lose control.

My hand began to move more quickly, and my lips went lower as I let him slip further into my mouth. His moans became louder, and his hips thrust more. I'd begun to keep my mouth in place as he pushed his cock deeper, even touching the back of my throat a time or two.

I'd only just begun to really enjoy Angel's need when I felt a hand in my hair. The sheet was thrown back to reveal a smiling man with hunger in his eyes. I glanced back at him and slowly pushed his cock down my throat until my nose pressed against his pubic bone. I heard him groan as his fingers wrapped themselves in my hair.

He thrust upward, ignoring the fact that I could not go any lower and hoping he could get another fraction of an inch down my throat. Gagging sounds escaped me as he held me down for a few seconds.

Then he pulled my head up slowly until his cock slipped from my lips. Drool ran down my chin as I smiled at him. "Such a little slut," he said.

I didn't say anything, and he wrapped his other hand in my hair before positioning my face over his cock. Slowly, he forced my face down, holding me there until I started to gag. Then he'd let me up enough to take a breath or two before pushing me back down.

Over and over again, he fucked my face. Never enough to make him cum, and never enough to make me hurt. Just enough to make a growing puddle of spit at the base of his cock.

Finally, he let me go and said, "Get on your hands and knees, slave." I didn't hesitate, didn't let him lose the need that pushed him to lose that control he clung too so tightly.

I turned around and faced away from him, and he knelt behind me. His hands gripped my ass regardless of the bruises. He enjoyed hurting me, and that was fine with me.

His cock pressed against my lips, begging to be allowed entrance, but he was already regaining some of his normal control. Instead of thrusting into me, he began to slap my ass. The room filled with sound of his hand on my bruised flesh mixed with my moans.

That red lightning raged inside of me as I took his pain. Searing pain and sensuous ecstasy twisted and turned inside of me, forcing my body to shake and writhe under his hand as I did everything in my power to prevent the orgasm from rushing through me.

Then the sounds stopped, and I looked back at the man who owned me. His face was focused on his handiwork, the deep red that he'd painted my ass. Swollen and throbbing, it enthralled him, and his eyes began to glaze over with lust.

He gripped his cock in one hand as his other went to my waist. Fingers tightened on my hip, and I knew what would happen next. He wasn't going to let my body try to get away. He wasn't going to allow me control anything.

He was going to use me like the fuck toy that I was. He thrust into me. I'd been wet. I'd been ready. That didn't change anything though. Agony poured into my body as his hips slammed into my thighs.

His other hand immediately went to my hips to hold me still as I tried to get away from the fire burning inside me. My body instinctively tried to jump forward, but there was no way out of his grip. Even as I screamed, he pulled back and did the same thing again. And again. My body tried to get away each time, but there would be no release from his grasp.

Over and over again, he used me like the slave that I was. I'd given myself to him, and though pain raged inside me, that wall that I'd built inside myself to hold my orgasms back was crumbling. Thrust after thrust, my willpower was failing.

Over my screams, he growled, "That's a good slave. Hurt for me." How could he expect me to control my body when he was tormenting me like this?

My body stopped trying to get away as I focused on controlling the orgasm that desperately needed an outlet. The pressure was becoming too much. His fingers released my waist and went to my ass, spreading it. They dug into my bruises, and he ignored the cries that escaped my lips.

Angel only cared about the pleasure that he was getting from using my body, and that fact only made it more difficult to keep the impending orgasm in check. I didn't think I could handle anymore, was tempted to give in and let the punishment come.

Then he said through labored breaths, "Cum for me, slave. Cum for me." The wall collapsed, and I screamed a single time as the waves washed over me. My body tried to force him out of me, but he ignored it as he continued to slam into me as hard as he could.

Then I heard him grunt behind me as I struggled under him. His hands still held onto my ass as he filled me with his cum. He didn't stop thrusting in and out of me until he was completely finished. His hands relaxed and released me, and I collapsed under him.

My body still shook from the combination of pain and pleasure coupled with the massive orgasm that had ripped through my body. He laid down next to me and held me tightly against his body. He was still trying to catch his breath when he said, "You're perfect. In every way."

It was hard to talk right after that. My body was still riding the high of it all, but I managed to say, "Thank you, Master." As I caught my breath, I heard him snoring already and I laughed a little.

Even after all of that, my body was beginning to come to life, no longer filled with that desperate need. I didn't want a nap even though Angel's strong arms felt wonderful. I wanted to feel the water on my body, wanted to feel the freedom of my swim. I pulled away from him and got out of bed to clean myself up.

When I got back, Angel was still snoring like normal. He always napped after he'd satisfied that hunger in the back of his eyes. He'd be up soon enough to cook breakfast though.

I felt filled with energy, and though I was sore, I couldn't help to smile. I was happy, truly and completely happy. Everything was right in the world, and my sore body just reminded me that I had a man that could bring me that kind of happiness.

I walked out of the room and down a hall to the living room. I flexed my calves as I walked, feeling the muscles that had grown up and down my legs. I hadn't been swimming long, and already I'd built enough muscle to be able to visibly see a difference.

I'd always been petite, but that had mostly been because of the specific diet that I'd been on. I wasn't allowed snacks or sweets or extra at mealtime. During our escape, Angel had pushed me to eat what I wanted and however much I wanted. I'd begun to feel a little softer than normal, but that was all gone.

Instead, my muscles, all of them, were getting harder and more apparent. Angel had been right. I would be ready. As long as I continued with my training, I'd be ready to pit my body against the ocean.

I walked out of the living room to the back porch where the pool began. I walked down the stairs to let my body get used to the cool water. This was my time. Angel never bothered me while I was in the pool. He never talked to me or asked to use my body. He never acknowledged me while I swam.

The water flowed over my body as I pushed forward. Steadily, I swam back and forth through the clear water. My end goal was thirty-two times without stopping. Last night, I'd done twenty-two. This morning I was going to twenty-three.

My lungs began to burn by the time that I got to eighteen. My shoulders ached at twenty. My left leg cramped at twenty-two.

None of it mattered though. I had to get twenty-three. No warm-up. No stretching. No goggles. Just get into the water and swim.

When I got to the end of twenty-three, I grabbed the edge and panted breathlessly. I was going to survive. I'd survived all this time. I wasn't going to let the ocean kill me. Not when I was this close to being free.

I smiled brightly. Nine more and I'd be at thirty-two. I'd do twenty-four tonight, and then it was only eight more increases. Four more days, and I'd be where I needed to be.

My body ached. It hurt everywhere. Every day. I'd thought that the pain in the cage had been bad, but

I could blame that on someone else. I'd done this to myself. I was the only one that I could be mad at for this pain.

Instead, I was proud. I'd grown a lot since we'd gotten to the farmhouse. I walked into the living room and grabbed a towel from the shelf next to the door to dry my naked body off.

"How many laps did you get this morning?" Angel's voice called out from the kitchen. I walked toward the voice and the scent of green onion and fried ham and eggs overcame me.

"Twenty-three," I said as I looked around the kitchen to see what Angel was making. Omelets. It was one of his favorite breakfast foods, and he was damned good at them.

"My leg cramped after twenty-two, but I finished." Angel nodded as he flipped one side of the omelet onto the central section.

"It hurt a lot, but I just let it float while I finished. I didn't want to let pain stop me from finishing."

"That's good. You need to teach your body that failing isn't a possibility. Whatever you set your goal as, you need to hit that. You need to be realistic, but once the goal is set, don't let pain or frustration or anything stop you from hitting it."

"Yes sir," I said. It hadn't been a command, but I said the words before I'd thought about it. It had just seemed natural.

"Do you want to go horseback riding today?" he asked, already knowing the answer.

I gave him a wide grin and said, "What do you think?"

"Will your legs be able to handle it and the hand-to-hand training and the night swim?" he asked, his voice showing genuine concern.

He was right to ask. My body was showing some signs of being overworked. The swimming would have been a lot in itself, but Angel had been fucking me constantly. If he wasn't using me, then we were doing martial arts training or horseback riding.

"Maybe I shouldn't go riding today." The thought was saddening. I knew that I wouldn't get to ride when we got to Florida. I wanted to get as much time on the horses as possible.

He slid the omelets onto plates and shut off the heat to the stove. I followed him to the table. "How about I give you a reprieve on the training and you give in to a day without a ride? Then you can let your body get a full day's rest other than the swimming."

I sighed. "Okay, but maybe you could go a little lighter on the sex, too?"

"I was planning on it. Especially after this morning. I feel especially satisfied after that. You really know how to make me happy, Maia."

I took a bite of the omelet and let the flavors wash over my tongue. God, this man was a good cook.

"I had to do something. I needed to cum so badly. So, so, so badly." I took another bite of the omelet.

"Well, what would you like to do instead?" I asked when I was finished chewing.

"We only have a week left. We could do some internet house hunting and shopping. There are a lot of things you'll want as soon as you get to Florida. Things like clothes and an apartment and cleaning supplies. All those things that will be a little tricky to get until you have a car."

My eyes went wide at his suggestion. "You're going to buy me all of that stuff?"

Angel grinned. "Of course. I'm not going to drop you off in a city you've never been to and just let you fall on your face."

"Well, how do you do internet shopping?"

Chapter 19: Longing

*Fearing change is simply a love for
yourself, for every change is a death. You
may know that you'll be reborn, but the
person you were will be gone forever.
When the war is done, the soldier dies
and the farmer is born.*

His cock was already throbbing. Angel's hands were in
my hair, but he wasn't doing any of the work. Every
day after I'd woken him up with my mouth, he'd
expected me to suck his cock before I left the bed. It
was a small thing in reality. He cooked breakfast and
cleaned up breakfast, and that usually took longer and
took more work.

How could I complain about sucking his cock
when he did so much? I bobbed up and down on it,
letting it slide down my throat occasionally. It wasn't
the rough sex that happened at night. It was just a
quick morning blowjob.

It still made my pussy wet, and it still made Angel
moan, but I was pretty sure that he had me do it so that
I started the day with a wet pussy.

Up and down. Up and down. Over and over again, I moved my head in a slowly increasing rhythm. One hand massaged his balls while the other stroked the shaft.

He groaned and pushed my head down lower, forcing me to take him into my throat. He began to cum, and I swallowed it down.

He released me and smiled at me. As always, he laid back down and enjoyed his post orgasm nap. He hadn't gotten out of bed yet, but he always enjoyed a short nap after he came.

I got out of bed and used the restroom. The routine was set, and I knew what to do without thinking. Next, it was time for my morning swim. I walked through the house and out the back door.

This time was strange though. Normally, I would walk out the door, and then I'd walk down the steps into the water. Then I'd swim my thirty-two laps and get out to eat breakfast with Angel.

Today was different.

I stood with the back door open, looking at the pile of gear that sat between the door and the stairs into the pool. I was barely awake, and I didn't know how to handle the difference.

Angel appeared behind me. "Today is different," I said softly. He put his hands around my waist and held me close to him.

"Tomorrow, we start the journey to Florida. You have to learn how to use scuba diving equipment." I turned to him, confused.

"I know. I told you that we were going to swim from the boat to an island. I needed you to be safe no matter what happened. I had you train without the scuba gear so that if something fails, you'll still be fine.

"We're going to scuba dive to the island?" I asked, still completely confused.

"We're going to get lowered into the water in scuba gear. Then we're going to swim under the water to an island. Swimming under the water means that other boats won't see us. The thing is that we only get one chance. If your equipment fails, if your oxygen tank isn't filled up or your goggle strap busts or your flipper breaks, then you can still do it."

"If you'd only trained enough to do it with scuba gear, then if something bad happened, you'd be in trouble."

I nodded. That made sense. Always prepare for the worst. It had become one of Angel's catch phrases. "And today, you're going to show me how all of it works?" I asked.

He nodded. It was a better plan than just swimming. Angel knew what he was doing.

"I'm going to miss this," he said.

"Me too. I'm going to miss it a lot."

"It's been so peaceful. Food, swimming, horses, and fucking. No stresses and no world. Just peacefully enjoying the good things in life."

"We could always stay here." I looked at him. "I'd stay here with you."

He shook his head. "I wouldn't be happy here for long. I can't stay in one place, and eventually people would find us. I've pissed too many people off for too long to be safe anywhere without a lot of people and a lot of guns."

"It is a nice dream, though," he said, and I sighed. It was a nice dream.

"Well, if we're still going to Florida, you'd better show me how to put all this stuff on."

Angel trotted along on Gray in front of me as we made the same laps around the farm that we'd made nearly every day. I rode Eeyore, and he complained the entire time. I liked the way that he seemed annoyed at everything I pushed him to do. It was so human.

Most people who rode horses wouldn't have considered our path to be of any interest. There was nothing to jump, and there wasn't beautiful scenery. Like Angel said, it just felt good to be away from everything human, to be natural again.

I patted Eeyore's neck and said, "This is our last ride, old man. How about we see how fast you can go?" He whinnied like normal and shook his head.

"Well that's too bad. Today, maybe you'll be the tired one and I'll go to sleep without shaking thighs." I squeezed my legs together tightly and leaned forward. He knew what I wanted, but he didn't want to give it to me. He never did.

Eeyore was well trained though. Snarly and cantankerous, but still well-trained and well-behaved. He jumped forward and raced along the path. I held myself against him, feeling his muscles work, and I watched the trees pass by.

Everything was a blur when he galloped. It wasn't jarring and bouncy like the trot. It was flying, a whir of motion below me that let me move faster than humans should be able to move. There was nothing in the world that felt like that. Nothing.

Across the pasture, we hurtled like a bullet out of a gun. My hair whipped around me, and I screamed. Not from pain. Not from pleasure. Just to scream. Just to feel the sound leave me.

The horse kept running. I nudged him back towards the main path that Angel was still on, and he slowly made the circle, still galloping. I reined him in, slowing his gallop well before we got to Angel and Gray.

Eeyore was breathing hard, and I saw bits of froth around his mouth. He didn't like to run, and I was sure that George, the owner of the farmhouse almost never actually got him up to a gallop.

"That was a good one, Eeyore," I said, out of breath myself. I hadn't pushed him very much in the past few weeks. He was old, and he hated galloping, so I had enjoyed the simple freedom of the wind in my hair as we walked and trotted on the path. Plus, I was usually already tired by the time I was riding him.

"It's time that we headed back to the stable, Maia," Angel said seriously. "We need to get them brushed down, and then we need to clean up the house. Tomorrow morning, we're leaving before dawn."

"Okay," I said as I looked down at Eeyore. It would be the last time I was on a horse for the foreseeable future, and it would definitely be the last time that I rode him.

"I'll miss you," I said, and he whinnied back at me. He chewed on the bit and shook his head.

Angel led us back to the stable, and I wondered what life would be like back in the real world. No one would know my past, and they wouldn't understand the hell that I'd been through. I'd have a fresh start, a life without the stains of Marcos and my time in Mexico.

The scars would still be there. The brand would still cross my skin, a trophy of surviving a world without kindness. No one else would understand that.

I'd never be able to tell them what had happened to me. They'd think I was lying. Angel had already explained that to me.

People knew about sex trafficking, but they didn't believe that it could happen to someone they knew. They knew that every once in a while someone would survive and return to the normal world, but if I tried to tell them that I was one of them without any proof, they'd think I was crazy. Then I'd either have to live with that or I'd have to prove it and cause all kinds of trouble for myself.

Angel had said that I could get plastic surgery to remove the brand, but I didn't want that. Not really. I couldn't erase the past, and this wasn't a symbol of the pain and terror. It was a symbol of my triumph, my victory over the monster who had killed my mother. I didn't want to get rid of it, to erase it like it hadn't happened.

No, I would just have to lie. I'd say that I'd been a consensual sex slave to a boyfriend when I was eighteen. That I'd been an idiot teenager with an older man, and I'd made a mistake. They'd probably just get turned on by the idea. Men liked the idea of sex slaves. Even Angel did.

When we got to the stable, I got off Eeyore and looked him in the eye. "You've been a good horse. I'll never forget you." He nuzzled my cheek and I giggled.

Angel led the horses into their stalls and I sat and watched. Things were changing, and I was afraid again. I wouldn't stop the process. I wouldn't run away from the changes, but that didn't mean that they didn't terrify me.

Chapter 20: Silence

The story of our life is written on our bodies and souls in scars. We are born with a blank canvas, and the world writes the novel of our lives from a pain-filled bottle of ink.

The wind whipped the air as we stood on the top of the cargo ship. Connex boxes covered the deck of the massive ship. Hundreds of them with different colors and labels. They were bound for Tampa Bay, just like us. We just had a short detour to take so that we could bypass customs.

We were dressed in the same uniforms that the rest of the crew was, but we weren't part of them. Instead, while they had their pre-docking meeting, we changed into the scuba gear next to the basket that hung over the side of the ship.

The first mate of the ship, a man with a generally unhappy demeanor to go along with a sour face and a long dark beard of curls, walked over to us. He was still in his uniform, a blue set of coveralls with various emblems emblazoning it.

"You're not going to get lost, are you?" he said to Angel as he eyed me with a smirk.

"I already paid you and your captain, so it shouldn't matter if we get lost and die out there," Angel replied with a straight face.

"It don't matter to me, but the captain says to remind you that if you get lost and picked up, you'd better not tell anyone you were on our boat."

"Javier, don't worry about me. This isn't my first rodeo, and if I failed simple plans like this, I wouldn't have become successful enough to pay that ridiculous bribe your captain required. All you have to do is drop us into the water, haul up the basket, and get rid of our clothes. Then you go home and enjoy your money. Buy some whores and liquor. Maybe they'll finally give you a reason to smile."

"Just get into the basket so we can be done with this." He turned around and lit a cigarette, making sure that no one was watching.

We'd been on the boat for two days. Both of us had hidden in our cabin during the trip, trying not to be seen by anyone that could remember us or report us, but we'd worn our uniforms the entire time just in case.

I stood up with my flippers and wetsuit on along with the air tank, and I stepped into the basket. Angel followed me, and we sat down in the center with our fins outward. The basket began to lower into the water, and I watched as the ocean slowly got closer and closer.

It was a clear blue, and I could see fish swimming under us as we got closer. A part of me was ecstatic that I'd be able to swim in the ocean with fish, but the other part of me was terrified by what Javier had said.

I trusted Angel. I had to. He hadn't led us wrong yet.

The netting that we sat on touched down on the water and the basket collapsed. I set the regulator into my mouth and gave it a few test breaths before taking the plunge into the warm water. I looked at Angel who pointed in a direction, and I followed him.

The water was crystal clear this far out, and I could see hundreds and thousands of fish around me. Most of them didn't even seem to notice us until we were right next to them. It was beautiful. I reminded me of the moment that I'd stepped into the pool three weeks ago and felt that freedom and pressure. This was the same way.

The difference was that I didn't have to go to the surface. Instead, I could sit in the silence of the ocean and feel that freedom of nothing and everything all at the same time without any rush to get a breath.

Looking down into what looked like a never-ending abyss was disconcerting, but I was too caught up in the freedom to pay much attention to it. Even though I was enjoying the sights and freedom, I never strayed far from Angel. I had no idea where we were going, and so I needed to stay close to him.

We swam for what seemed like no time at all, but soon enough, we weren't looking into the abyss, and instead were looking at sandbars with moss and grasses. The water was still clear here, but there was a sandy tint to it.

We stayed under the water all the way until we got to the actual land. Then we stood up and walked to the shore. The island was covered in palm trees and grass, and it was larger than I'd expected. Not just a speck of sand in the middle of the ocean, this was an island that someone could have put a house and a garden on.

No one would have paid to visit it, but I could see someone wanting to live away from the rest of the world on it. I guess it was just too far away from the real world to be a viable place to put a house. Regardless, it was perfect for what we needed.

We walked into the forest of palm trees and overgrown grasses and sat down to take off our tanks and most of our gear.

"Stay down below the level of the grass, Maia. Remember that this island is well known by the Coast Guard, and when they pass it, they'll look at it to make sure that there aren't people here. As long as we stay below the grass level, no one will be able to see us, but they'll be looking for heads.

"We're almost there, Maia. Are you ready?" he asked.

I shook my head softly. "No, but I'll never be ready. You never really think you're ready until you do something this drastic. I wasn't ready to be rescued. I wasn't ready to ride a horse. I wasn't ready to scuba dive or be shot at or be branded. I survived all of them, and I'll survive this regardless of how afraid I am."

Angel put his hand on my thigh. "You're wrong, Maia. You're ready to be in the real world. I've seen you go from scared little girl to grown woman in the past month. You're going to be okay."

I sighed. "Maybe. Maybe you're right. I have changed a lot in the past month, haven't I?"

He nodded and pulled me in for a hug. "I'm going to miss you. Not just the sex, even though that's been pretty amazing."

"I'm going to miss you too," I said quietly. "And not just the sex either. You'll always be my hero, but I like you too. You make me smile and laugh. And there's your cooking..."

He hugged me again, and we were quiet. He laid down on the sand and looked up at the sky, and I laid down on his shoulder.

"The boat will be here after dark," he said.

"We could just stay here, Angel. Our last chance for it to just be us." I heard him sigh deeply.

"I wish it could just be us. We can't just leave the world behind." I didn't respond. I couldn't. I knew that he told me these things, but I didn't really understand why we couldn't run away from it all. We could pretend to just be foreigners in a faraway land and live a simple life.

I guess that wasn't what he wanted from life though. He wanted that life more than he wanted me.

I closed my eyes as I lay on his shoulder, and I felt the sadness begin to creep into me. I wanted to be free of Mexico once and for all, but I hated the fact that I would also be forced to live without Angel.

I let my exhaustion take over, and I let my mind let go. The wind in the trees and the waves on the shore filled my mind with sounds that meant peace, and before long, I was snoring.

"Maia, the boat's here."

I blinked my eyes a few times and turned to see Angel smiling at me. "How long has it been?" I asked.

"A few hours, but we need to get going. No one can see that boat on this island, or we're going to have problems."

I nodded and got up quickly. Angel stood up and jogged out to the water where a personal offshore fishing boat was waiting. I followed behind him. The boat waited in the water only about fifty feet out, and a rope ladder hung over the side. Without saying anything, Angel began swimming out to it, and I followed.

He was treading water when I made it to the boat. "Climb up. I'll be right behind you," he said. Without needing any extra prodding, I began climbing. When I got to the edge, two men wearing sunglasses helped me into the boat. One wore a plain red T-shirt and jeans while the other wore a fishing shirt and khaki shorts.

"Get out of the wetsuit," Angel said as soon as he got on board and began to unzip his own. He handed his suit to one of the men who folded it up and stuffed it into a cargo area. I handed him mine as well, and I glanced at his face out of the corner of my eye. For the briefest of moments, I could have sworn that I'd seen him before except that he was wearing a white button up shirt instead of the red shirt. Then the image was gone, and I was left wondering where I might have seen him.

The man handed me a small bag of clothes, and I began to put them on over the one-piece swimsuit that I was wearing. A pair of capris and a T-shirt with the image of a restaurant on it. Then I put on the foam sun visor and sunglasses. Angel was already dressed in a fishing shirt and jean shorts. He pulled out a wallet and two rings from his bag.

He handed me a ring and smiled. The ring was white gold. Filigree and diamonds covered it like thin vines holding crystalline fruit, and in the center was a square cut diamond with more vines curling up to hold it in place, slightly above the rest of the ring. It was beautiful, more beautiful than any ring I'd ever seen. "Will you be my wife for the next three hours, Maia?" I grinned. "Of course, dear husband. But why do we need to be married for three hours?"

"It just adds to the story if anything happens. You're mostly safe already, but we don't want any trouble. Always prepare for the worst."

I nodded and put on the ring. It felt heavy, but also very right to wear the ring. The boat roared to life, and I sat down on the cushioned seat. It was going to be a long ride.

I looked down at my hand, at the ring that was only an illusion. I'd spent the past month with a man who was perfect for me in every way. I was wearing a ring he'd given me. He'd stolen me away, my knight in black armor, and now he was leaving me.

It wasn't his fault. Or mine. It just was the way it had to be, but that didn't take the pain away. It didn't make me want that weight on my finger to be permanent any less.

It was too short. All of it. This was the end of the trip, the end of the little bubble that Angel and I had lived in for the last month. This was the end of not only the bubble, but also the end of us.

A tear slid down my cheek as the wind whipped past us. I hadn't expected to hate this moment so much, and for the first time in my life, I couldn't just ignore it. I needed to feel the pain. It was like the brand. I didn't want to forget it. I wanted to remember the anguish.

Chapter 21: Instructions

A woman's life changes in silence. The
most important moments, the ones that
matter more than anything happen
without any fanfare, without any parades.
They happen with soft whispers, a wiped
tear, and a slowly closing door.

*Y*ou start work the day after tomorrow. It'll help
you to build a strong routine, Maia." I tried to
pay attention to Angel as I sat in the chair across from
him at his desk. It was so damned difficult to think of
anything except the impending loneliness.

"Your apartment is all set up with the clothes we
bought and plenty of food. Until you get your license,
you can get your groceries delivered. I showed you
how to find things on the internet, and if you need
anything while I'm gone, just ask Tony."

I looked at Tony who sat next to me. He was a
quiet man in a suit. Quiet and stout. He looked like a
gorilla in a human costume, complete with all the extra
hair. It seemed to come out of the sides of his cuffs
and his neckline. Plus, his beard was massive.

Angel took a deep breath and let it out slowly. "Maia, I know that I'm not leaving your life entirely, but you need to start building a real life. One without me. That means you need to find other people, including other men. I'm not trying to tell you what to do, but you probably should try dating."

It took me a moment to realize what he was saying. He wanted me to leave him behind. Already. It was too soon, too fast. All of it.

"Okay," I said, and he looked at me, that seriousness filling his face.

"What?" he asked. He could see it. The pressure that threatened to force me into tears.

"I just didn't think you'd be leaving already. I thought you'd be here a little longer before you had to go." Angel looked at Tony and motioned for him to give us some privacy.

The large man nodded and stood up without a sound, leaving us alone in the room.

"Maia, I hadn't expected to be away for a month. This job was pushed as much as it could be. I was supposed to do it two weeks ago, and the people I'm working with have been more understanding that I'd expected. In the world I live in, once you take a job, you do the job or bad things happen."

I nodded. "I understand that. It's just..." I tried to hold back the tears that threatened to fall. "I'm all alone here, Angel. I know that I can call Tony, but it's not the same. I don't know him. I don't know anyone. What if the Cartel finds me? What if I can't figure out the internet stuff, and I run out of food?"

Angel sat back in his chair with his arms crossed. "Maia, you have to stop being so afraid of what ifs. You're as safe as I can make you. You're going to be fine. It's going to be hard. You already knew that, but it's going to be fine. You just have to do the best you can."

"I'll be home in about a week, and then we can chat again about everything. If something terrible happens like the Cartel finds you or you run out of food, you can call Tony. He's more than capable of taking care of things like that."

He looked at me and saw the fear and pain that raced through my eyes. He stood up, shoving the chair back as he walked around the desk to stand right in front of me. I'd never seen him angry. Not like this.

"Don't you know that this is hard for me too? I don't want to leave you. I don't want to let you go. Ever. But we both agreed that you were better off without me. I have to let you go. I have to find my life again. No matter how hard it is for either of us, we can't just pretend like we're still in Mexico."

"All I can bring you is more pain. You can be free of that here. You can be free of the suffering of the life that I live in. I'm willing to hurt so that you can be free. Can't you do the same?"

I nodded again and stood up, making a decision. "Then can you have Tony take me to my apartment? I need to start figuring out my life, Angel, and being with you doesn't help."

I'd never felt more alone. In my cage, I'd been alone, but I hadn't known any better. Not since my mother had died in front of me. I'd felt alone for the first few months, but I'd been a child then. I'd changed the way that I thought. My mind had been able to adapt.

Now, I'd adapted to having Angel by my side. I'd adapted to having him as my hero, my boyfriend, my Master. I was alone now. I was safe, and I was able to be a normal person, but I was all alone.

I pulled the ring off my finger and gave him a half-smile. "Our three hours are up I guess." I tossed the ring onto his desk.

I turned to leave the room and felt my pants rub against my brand.

Chapter 22: Solitude

Silence isn't the lack of sound. It's the deafening sound of nothing where something should be. The sound of a windless night when there should be a breeze. The sound of no birds when they'd been there the day before. The sound of an empty home where a lover's voice once was.

The air was crisp and clean. No scent of anything. No smog, no trash, no nothing. Also, no horses, no pool, no Angel. I sighed as I looked at the city below my fourth-floor apartment. I didn't remember it being like this. Constant noise coming from the world below, and nothing that mattered.

How could the world be so filled with noise, so filled with people, and yet feel so lonely? It just didn't make sense.

I walked back inside. How many times had I walked this simple and short path? I needed more room to stretch my legs. Tomorrow I started my first job, a veterinarian technician. In short, I'd be cleaning dog and cat kennels and wiping down rooms.

It was a job that didn't require any experience, and it was one that wouldn't expect a lot out of me. I would be given my jobs and I could do them without any real person to person contact which was fine by me. I still didn't like the idea of being around so many people.

I walked to the freezer and pulled out the TV dinner that I was going to eat tonight. Some kind of pasta with chicken dinner. I read the directions and followed them. The microwave whirred loudly, and I pulled out a steaming bowl of something.

Steam rose from it, but the smells didn't make me long to taste it, didn't make me desperate to ignore the world so that I could only smell it more strongly. This was food that normal people ate. I was not impressed.

I took a bite and was just as unimpressed by it. Bad noodles that were overcooked were mixed with overcooked chicken bites in a simple white sauce. This wasn't what I'd become accustomed to, but it was what I had.

I'd been right about being forced to learn to cook. I couldn't live on TV dinners. I would prefer the mush in the cage to this. I ate it anyway. I knew that I needed the food. Just like I'd eaten what I was given in the cage.

"Fuck it," I said as finished the last of the pasta. I tossed the container in the trash and dropped the fork in the sink as I walked to the bedroom. I stripped off my clothes, clothes that still made me itch. Especially the bra. I did not enjoy the feeling of something holding my breasts like that. And that damned wire...

I pulled a one-piece swimsuit out of one of the drawers and quickly put it on. I wasn't going to the pool for anyone else. I didn't need eyes on me. I just needed the water. I needed something from the days in Mexico. Something to remind me that the world hadn't ended when I'd climbed on that boat.

I rode the elevator down to the second floor which held the indoor pool of the apartment complex. I strode through the glass doors fully expecting to swim my thirty-two laps.

And I stopped. Children played in the pool, splashing and playing like children do. Their laughter bounced off the walls, sending echoes of happiness that brought only frustration to me.

It wouldn't have mattered anyway. The pool was too small. Not even a quarter of the size of the one that I'd spent so much time in. This was not a pool that I'd ever use. Not for swimming at least. I gritted my teeth. They weren't breaking the rules. I should be happy that the children were enjoying themselves, but I couldn't get over the fact that nothing, not even the pool was right.

I turned around without even leaving the doorway and walked back to the elevator. I just wanted to scream. Why couldn't I still be in Mexico? What in this world was worth the frustration and the loneliness?

I walked down the hall to my door. A man from across the hall stepped out of his door at about the same time.

"Evening, miss," he said. His eyes roamed over my body as all men's do, but it was a quick glance even though I was in a skintight swimsuit.

"Evening," I said back, and he continued to walk down the hall to the elevator. I unlocked my door and went into my apartment, trying my best not to explode loud enough to have people banging on my door.

There was nowhere in this world to let out a scream. Even in my cell, I'd been able to scream. I could just let the emotions out. On the farm, it had been the same way. I could go outside and just scream, but not here. Not in this world.

I tried to bottle them up as best as I could. Eventually, I would find a place to let them loose. I would find a way to release all the frustration that raged inside of me. I tried to relax in the bed, but I couldn't find a comfortable position.

I was alone, so at least I could take these clothes off. I pulled the swimsuit off me and left it on the floor and crawled back into the bed. I turned the fan on, and that reminded me of Mexico.

Then I turned the air conditioner up to eighty degrees and threw the comforter on the ground. Just a sheet and a fan were all I needed. I needed that thin sheen of sweat on my body. I needed to be able to close my eyes and imagine that same sheen on Angel's body.

Falling asleep wasn't easy, but there was nothing else to do. I'd tried television, but the shows hadn't made very much sense. I knew that I could get onto the computer and try to set up the movie stuff that Angel had explained, but it just didn't sound like anything I was interested in.

Sleep was the only thing that sounded good. At least in dreams I could go back to Mexico. Back to Eeyore and Gray. Back to simple and solitude. Back to good food. Back to Angel.

Chapter 23: Salt

The fading feel of her hand, of her lips, of her breath. The whispering words of goodbye. The memories of their nights together. That was all that the wanderer had to remember her by.

The waves rose and fell on the Atlantic that morning, and I sat and watched them. The men worked around me, their poles resting as they fished. This was not the best of tuna fishing spots outside of San Diego, but it wasn't an unfished area. That was why it was perfect, and it was why I'd used it so many times in the past.

Alonzo, the captain came up to me as I sat on a pile of boxes. "What time is that boat supposed to be here?" he asked.

I shrugged my shoulders. "It'll be here today. It's not like you'll miss it." The cargo ship was massive, carrying all variety of goods from Vietnam. As a side item, it carried thirty million dollars worth of heroin, about a hundred pounds of it. The crew of the cargo ship didn't know about that, but this crew did.

"Angel, we can't just sit all day in the same spot. That's not how tuna boats work." I smirked at him.

"Maybe not, but that's exactly how smuggling boats work. Today, your fucking tuna fishing matters about as much as your wife's sagging tits. You've been bitching all morning about how we need to move, how we need that boat to hurry up. That's just not how this works. Problems happen on big ships like that, and we have to be the agile ones, so until a real problem occurs, we just sit tight."

Alonzo gritted his teeth. He wanted to argue. I knew he wanted to tell me about how we were going to blow our cover, and he wasn't wrong. Tuna fishermen didn't sit like this, not when they weren't catching fish. Luckily, there weren't many boats in the area because it wasn't a great spot.

He also knew that he didn't want to piss me off. I could have convinced a different boat and a different crew to do this exact same thing, and he wouldn't be getting paid a hundred thousand dollars. That was a huge sum of money for Alonzo. In fact, it was probably close to as much as he made in a good year from fishing.

"Alright, Angel. We'll keep sitting here. I just hope that no one notices us doing something stupid. I've made it a point to do very few stupid things in my life, so people might take notice if we stay here for too long." He was calming down which was a good thing. For him, and for me.

"Maybe you should start doing a few more stupid things on occasion. That way I don't have to find a different, stupider crew next time I need to pick up a package in the middle of the Atlantic Ocean."

He nodded and left me alone on my boxes. He was antsy. The whole crew was. The prison time for being involved in this bit of smuggling would be a decade minimum for every single one of them. Thirty million dollars of heroin was a lot of heroin. I got a cool ten percent of that. The Russians had paid the Vietnamese just about 8 million for it, so they'd be up nineteen million after they liquidated it.

Not a bad deal for any of us. The crew would get a hundred and fifty thousand for their trouble, and the two men on the cargo ship would get another hundred. Everyone made out well.

As long as we didn't get caught.

I'd made my fortune doing things like this, and I'd never been caught. In fact, I still wasn't on any radars, even after all these years. The fact that I paid everyone well and chose people that would be grateful for the chance was one of the ways that I kept off the radar.

That and the fact that I didn't take shortcuts. Ever. Always be prepared for the worst was the motto

I lived by. It was something Francisco had instilled in me as he'd brought me up in the world.

I shouldn't have been frustrated at Alonzo. He had the same fears and frustrations that I did. The boat should have been here this morning at about dawn. Instead, it was almost two, and we hadn't seen anything. If my men on the cargo ship hadn't seen us, I'd have gotten a text, but there hadn't been one.

We used communication only when absolutely necessary. It could be traced, and that meant that we could be caught. The only reason they would have texted was to tell us that they'd dropped it without us there so that we'd know to get there ASAP.

Instead, we just needed to be patient. I didn't want to be patient. I wanted to be back in Tampa fucking Maia. We'd been gone for two days now, and I was more sexually frustrated than I could remember.

Not only that, but I was frustrated that we'd had to leave Mexico. That girl had actually made me laugh and smile and forget the world that I lived in. She'd been perfect. I'd had to force her away though. She couldn't have just stayed with me. It would have ruined everything that I'd worked for.

Now she'd have to learn to live in the world. She'd have to grow some more. I tried to push her to be independent while we were in Veracruz, but she didn't know how. Eventually, everyone has to be pushed into the deep end, or they'll always be afraid of it.

She'd been afraid of the real world. More than anyone I'd ever met. She had a reason for it, but good God, that girl never stopped stressing about bills and other ridiculous things. How many times had I been forced to reassure her that I'd make sure that she wouldn't starve to death?

The waves continued to roll. That was the way of the world wasn't it. It didn't matter how much you wanted something, the waves would always keep rolling. They'd keep rocking your boat. You couldn't fight them. You couldn't beat the world back. Instead, you just had to be patient and roll with them.

That's why I was sitting out on a boat in the middle of the ocean instead of in Tampa with Maia. The waves kept rolling. She would have to learn how to ride the waves without me, and I had to remember that even though I could do a lot of things, I couldn't control the ride.

I saw it then, the speck in the distance. I called out, "The boat's here." Two of the fishermen nearly dropped what they were doing even as they baited their hooks before they remembered that they were supposed to ignore everything.

The first mate ran over to where I sat and looked through his binoculars. "Yessir, that's the boat. Sure as shit. It's about fucking time, yeah?" he said without taking his eyes off the speck in the distance. "Thought I was gonna get another ulcer worrying about how fucked we were if we'd missed that damned boat."

The man had a way with words. "Me too. Me too. Go tell the captain before he gets one."

We'd pulled up our lines and waited as the boat passed just a little too close to us for most of the men's comfort. Waves rolled under us, larger than normal as the ship cut a trench in the ocean before it was quickly filled.

Then two boxes fell from the deck of the boat more than fifty feet in the air. Just two little boxes that had been sealed tight in a marine bag and attached to a floatation device. They would have been unnoticed if we weren't all looking for them.

As soon as the ship had passed enough for us to get the packages, the captain gunned the engine, racing to pick them up before something happened. It would be disastrous if we lost the packages. By disastrous, I meant that we'd all be dead.

Nothing disastrous happened though. Instead, the first mate used the gaff to hook the ring that had been installed on the float and pulled them up to the deck. No one touched them once they were on the deck until I opened the bag.

Small packages filled the bag. Each one was worth a million on the street. Little packages like something that your grandmother would bake and wrap in plastic before bringing it to a family get together.

"Good job everybody. Now get the fuck back to fishing. We've got to fill that cooler up before we can go home and celebrate. You haven't gone home without a full cooler in more than a year, and we aren't going to this time either."

The first mate gave me a relieved smile before barking orders at the rest of the crew. We were packing up our stuff and going to a good fishing spot. We were already halfway full.

"We're good?" he asked, and I nodded at him. "Let's get these into a hidey hole just in case we get a surprise inspection."

He nodded his head and grabbed a bag. I picked up the other. Only a few more days, and I'd be back home in Tampa. Then I could check in on Maia.

Chapter 24: Blood

The strength of a human is not how
much they can endure. Simply surviving
is done by every person on the planet.
Strength is what you see when you do
more than survive, when you stop
allowing the world to direct your actions.

I swept the floor of the back room of the vet clinic.
It was something I could do a hundred times a day and
there would always be more, but it was something to
occupy my hands. It was hard to find things to do
when I didn't know anyone or anything.

Even then, it was better to be here than at my
apartment. There was nothing at the apartment. I'd
started practicing the martial arts that Angel had been
teaching me at the farm, but I could only do it for so
long before it just became boring.

At least the exercise would keep my muscles
strong. I'd already found a swimming pool to swim in.
A twenty-four hour gym within walking distance had it,
and it was purely for swimming laps. I'd found it last

night, and since tomorrow was my day off, I was going to sign up then.

Angel had said that I didn't have to worry about money for a few months and to just buy what I needed. He was going to show me how to deal with money better when he got home, but I was already researching banks.

That was all that I had to do at home. I'd tried to watch Netflix, but I didn't understand most of the shows, and I didn't want to watch the shows that I did understand. I didn't need to see more violence. It didn't hold the romance for me that it held for most people.

Instead, I trained my body and I researched. Slowly but surely, I was beginning to get some confidence with my new life. Angel would be proud of me. I'd ordered groceries yesterday, and I had texted and answered phone calls. I was getting it, and the world wasn't quite as scary as I'd thought it would be.

I'd made real food and messed it up completely. I'd tried an omelet like Angel had made many times in front of me, but it had stuck to the pan, and then it had burned. I'd eaten it anyway, but it was nowhere near as good as his had been. Practice was all it would take, just like with the swimming. I just had to be willing to struggle initially, and I'd learn to do whatever I wanted.

I was still frustrated at most people though. They walked around full of anger at their lives. Lives full of loving family and nice houses and delicious foods. They still found things to be angry about. I didn't understand how they could be angry with their lives when I was happy with mine.

I had no one except Angel, and I still carried the brand from Marcos. Maybe the difference was that my life was getting better, and all of these other people's lives were stagnant. I wondered why they didn't just practice harder or care more about their goals.

That made all the difference in my life now that I was out of a cage, now that I was my own person. I set a goal and I worked towards it. Every day. I wanted to be able to protect myself, so I trained. I wanted good food, so I cooked. I wanted to learn about the world, so I researched.

"Hey Maia, just about quitting time, isn't it?" a voice said as I swept. I looked up at Dan, one of the other vet techs.

"Yeah, I think so." He stood a few feet away leaning against some of the kennels.

He was a soft man. Light brown hair that was long enough that it got messy when he worked hard, but not long enough to get in his way. His eyes sparkled with life, and he rarely had anything but a smile on his face. He was a good guy from everything I could see, and he tended to brighten everyone's day just by being in the room.

"What are you doing on your day off?" he asked.

I smiled back at him and said, "Signing up for a gym and going swimming. And trying to cook a steak."

"What gym?"

"I don't remember the name, but it's a few blocks from my apartment."

"Oh." There were a few moments of awkward silence, and I went back to finishing up the sweeping that I'd been doing.

"Well, I was wondering if you wanted to go to a movie tomorrow night. If you're too busy, that's cool, but I just thought that... Maybe?"

He was a nice guy. He was no Angel, but he was a nice guy. I had to distance myself from Angel. He'd said it. I'd said it. This was how I started doing that. Maybe he might even want to have sex, and I needed sex so badly that it was beginning to keep me up at night.

"That sounds great, Dan. You have my number, right?" I said it without putting the broom down.

His smile was from ear to ear. "Yeah, how about I pick you up at six for the movie and then we go to dinner afterward?"

"I'd like that."

"That's great. I've got to go finish up my stuff before I can go. I'll text you tomorrow, okay?" Excitement flooded his every word, and I couldn't help but let it cheer me up even more.

"Okay, I'll talk to you then."

He was gone, and I looked around. Everything I could do was done. Next week, I'd learn more stuff about how to help the vets, but for now, all the cleaning was done. I swept the fur into the dustpan and carried it to the trash.

I clocked out like I'd been shown how to do, and I left. Tomorrow was going to be a good day. Swimming, steak, and a date. I was doing this. I was becoming normal.

I walked down the street in the early evening. It was still summer, and the sun wouldn't be going down for another few hours, but it was cooling off. I couldn't see the heat waves off the concrete anymore like you could at two or three in the afternoon.

People walked beside me, and cars passed me, leaving the smell of exhaust in their wakes. I was a part of the city, part of the world that I'd left so long ago. No different from them. At least not where people could see.

Yet, for some reason, I didn't want to walk next to them. I didn't want to be another footstep in a million. I wanted to fly like I'd flown on Eeyore. I wanted to swim like I'd done in that pool.

Maybe tomorrow I'd be able to feel that again. Maybe I'd feel the same freedom when my feet touched the water, when it surrounded me with its comforting pressure. Or maybe this world would ruin it again. It seemed to ruin everything.

I didn't run. I didn't fly. I didn't swim. I just walked along the street like I'd been told to do. Follow what they do. Do what they do. Be one of them. Just another person in a huge city.

I walked all the way home, turning the corner and opening the door. A few steps to the elevator. A man stepped in behind me. Attractive with hard eyes that stared ahead and didn't look at me.

I pushed the fourth-floor button, and he looked down but didn't push a button. Seconds passed, and the elevator rose slowly with a groan. "Nice evening tonight," I said to the man.

"It is. It'll be better when it cools off a bit more, but it's not as bad as it has been." His voice was hard like his eyes, but the words weren't.

"Do you live on the fourth floor?" I asked.

"Just visiting someone." I glanced at him. He was large, not like Tony, my emergency contact, but larger than most men. Dark hair and dark eyes with a clean cut look to his face. He had an important job somewhere. He was probably one of those men that other people looked up to, hoping that they could be like him some day.

The door opened, and he motioned for me to go first. "Hope you have a good evening," I said as I walked down the hall to my apartment, fishing in my purse for my keys. As I put the key in the doorknob, I heard the man pass me, continuing on to a door further down the hall.

The lock clicked, and I opened the door. Suddenly, rough hands covered my mouth and gripped my waist, picking me up and forcing me through my doorway into my apartment. He kicked the door shut and headed to the back of the apartment towards my bedroom.

He whispered in my ear, "Just shut the fuck up and it'll be over quickly. If you struggle, I'll have to hurt you." I looked down at the cold steel of a long knife pressed against my neck. "Can you be a good little whore and keep your mouth shut?"

I'd known men like this since I was eleven years old. Men who wanted to dominate a woman when she didn't want him. I knew how to shut the fuck up and take it. I also knew that giving them what they wanted was the best way to minimize the pain.

I nodded, and he said, "Good. Take off your clothes."

My body shook just a little. Not enough that he'd notice. Not enough for anyone to notice. If I'd still been in the cage, I wouldn't have shaken at all. It would have been a normal day if I'd still been in the cage.

I wasn't in the cage though. I was free. I hadn't expected this. I hadn't thought that this would ever happen again. It didn't seem to matter where I was, evil would follow.

I let my pants fall to the ground, and I pulled my top off and dropped it to the ground. I didn't hesitate as I reached around to unclasp my bra, a plain black bra that matched the plain black panties that I wore.

The bra fell to the ground, and the man looked at my breasts like all men do. His eyes were just as hard as they'd been in the elevator, but lust flared in them. I pulled my panties down and stepped out of them. His eyes focused on my brand even before seeing my pussy.

He saw it for what it was. He knew that I was broken. He knew that I wasn't just a normal girl. And he smiled. The hardness intensified, and I knew that I should be scared.

I wasn't though. He wouldn't do anything that hadn't already been done. He couldn't. No one could. I'd seen the very worst of the world already. Anything this man did was just a confirmation that the world was filled with monsters.

I turned toward the bedroom, and the man followed, only a foot behind me. I looked at the rumpled sheet and the comforter on the floor before turning to the man who followed me.

He looked at my body, and the lust raged through him. He held the knife in one hand and ran his other hand over my body, starting at my collar bone and moving down to my breasts.

I could feel my body preparing itself for the rape. I could feel the wetness building and the blood rushing to my pussy. I knew the feeling so well. Just let it happen, and then he'll leave. Just like before.

His hand ran over the brand, feeling the curve of the letters and he smiled. The hardness of his eyes raced through him, a dark outline to an evil act. Just submit. Do what he wants. It's not any different than before.

His hand found my pussy, found the wetness building. "You want this, don't you?" He pressed his finger into my entrance, and his rough fingers scraped against my insides. I looked past him, to the wall behind him, and I tried to lose myself in my mind.

Everything inside of me began to rebel against it though. This wasn't the same. I wasn't in the cage. I wasn't a slave anymore. I wasn't just some toy that men rented for an hour anymore.

I was a person.

I may not be normal. I may have scars across my body and across my soul, but I was still a person. And those scars made me stronger, both my soul and my body.

Things happened so fast that I barely remembered them later. One moment, I was letting him finger me, and the next, Angel's training kicked in. I gripped the wrist holding the knife, and I twisted, forcing the knife to the floor.

The man's hand left my body to grab me, but I didn't care. He immediately tried to step backward, expecting me to kick his balls. No, Angel had explained that every man instinctively protected his balls, and that I'd have to be much faster than them.

Instead, I reached out with both hands, ignoring his attempts to hold me back. He could have hit me, could have done just about anything, and my movement wouldn't have stopped. My hands gripped both sides of his head at the temple.

Rage fueled me and training focused me. I would not be a slave. I would not be a toy, and I would not let the evil in the world hurt me anymore.

Never again.

I didn't scream. I just pushed. My thumbs pressed into the man's eyes, nails digging into his quickly closing eyelids.

He screamed though. Louder than I ever had. Even when I'd been hurt the first time, I didn't scream like this man. As I felt the soft pop under each thumb, I released his head.

His hands went to his eyes as he screamed in pain. I didn't stop. No, I would not allow this monster to survive. I picked up the knife he'd dropped and holding it like Angel had taught me, I moved without hesitation.

The steel disappeared and reappeared on the other side as it slipped through the flesh of his neck and a river of red poured down his dress shirt. The screaming stopped abruptly, and a gurgling sound replaced it.

I withdrew the knife, and his hands went to his neck. He was a dead man trying to breathe. I knew that. He knew that.

And I smiled. A cold rage-filled smile. There should have been words, but I was enjoying that gurgling sound too much to interrupt it.

I should have felt revulsion as I watched the man die. I should have felt pity or anger or something, but as the life flowed out of him, so did all of my feelings. I'd been filled with anger and rage and frustration for days, but now I finally felt calm.

I wasn't a normal person. I wasn't a slave either. I had been broken, but I'd put the pieces back together. The scars would always be there, but so would I. I'd survived, and I was stronger now.

I knew that many women have been broken this evening, but I wasn't. My soul was hardened against this. I was calloused and rough, but I was still whole.

It was like the final broken piece of me had slipped into place as I watched the river of red run across my carpet.

I didn't stop watching him until the blood stopped running. Then I stepped back and realized that I didn't know what to do. I had protected myself. I had stopped a man from raping me. I had killed a monster.

That didn't mean anything to the police though. This man had been important, and I had a slave brand. I had fake paperwork. I had only lived in my apartment for a week. All of it meant that I couldn't deal with the police. There was only one answer.

I walked back to where my purse lay on the ground right inside of my door. I pulled my phone out of it and dialed a number.

"Angel, are you back in town?" I asked softly.

"Yeah, I just got back about an hour ago. What's wrong?"

"What do you do with a dead body?"

Chapter 25: Pure

Sparks cannot turn into raging fires
without help. It doesn't take much. A
breath and a twig. A breeze and a scrap
of paper. But without that little nudge,
that little bit of help, it will die and turn
to ash without having seen the flame that
it could have been.

W hat happened?" Angel said as he looked at the river of blood and the body laying on my bedroom floor. His eyes were hollow sockets and a gaping hole split the flesh of his neck.

There was no anger in Angel's voice. No fear or frustration or even real concern over the fact that I'd killed a man.

"He tried to rape me," I said with only a bit of nerves giving my voice a soft quiver.

"And you killed him?"

"Yes."

Angel looked around the room, humming softly as he thought, and then he nodded to Tony. He took me by the shoulder and walked me into the bathroom.

"Take a shower. Wash the blood off and I'll put some clothes on the sink for you. Then go eat some dinner and spend some time away from the apartment. Come back in two hours. I shouldn't have to tell you this, but don't talk to anyone about it."

"Okay," I said still feeling a little numb from it all.

He left the bathroom, and I took off the robe that I'd been wearing while I waited for Angel. I turned the water as hot as it would get. I needed to wash the man's blood off me. I needed to be rid of anything to do with the monster.

Steam billowed out of the shower as I stepped into it. I just let it run down my back for a few moments, enjoying the way that it felt. The nearly scalding water seemed to do more than just wash the physical evidence away.

Soap was necessary to get physically clean, but the heat was what I needed to cleanse myself of the man's very presence. I wished that there was a way to burn it away with fire.

I ran my hands through my hair, remembering how long it used to be, and realizing that the blonde roots were showing again. I'd survived it all. I'd had to hide because we were running, but not anymore. I didn't need to hide from the monsters anymore.

Without trying to rush, I washed myself. When I stepped out of the shower and dried off, a long flowing dress was folded and sitting on the counter next to the sink. No bra and no panties.

Angel knew me so well. Other women would have wanted to cover up after what had happened, but my natural state was nakedness. I had to leave, but I didn't have to be uncomfortable. I let the dress settle over my slightly damp body and actually enjoyed it.

It fit my curves and was meant to be worn without any underwear. It was too tight on top to be worn with a bra, but it covered more than any of my other dresses. Black and red swirled together in strangely abstract image of roses on the front and long thin sleeves covered my arms.

It was beautiful, light, and yet comforting with its tightness. This wasn't one of my dresses though. Why would Angel have brought a new dress for me?

I didn't know and didn't care that much. Not with everything that was going on. I ran a brush through my hair, and I stepped out of the bathroom.

"I'm done," I said as Tony and Angel moved things into the room. Boxes of cleaners and what looked to be a vacuum cleaner. I slipped on a pair of leather sandals. They didn't really match, but that didn't matter to me right then.

"Good. Go get some food. Take your time. I'll be here when you get back." His eyes stayed on his task until he finished. Then he turned to me. "That dress looks incredible on you."

I smiled back at him, no longer worried about the body on the floor. "Thank you."

I stepped around the trails of blood in the carpet and left the apartment. I needed to be able to take my time with dinner. I walked down the hall to the elevator trying to think of a place that would help me feel better.

Nothing came to mind. I didn't even want to eat. There was only one thing I wanted to do. Swim. I needed the water. I needed the freedom. I needed to be back in Mexico right then.

I walked out of the apartment and followed the path in my mind. My steps were faster than normal, and I ignored the people that cluttered the sidewalk. It was strange that the sun was still out after what had happened. In my mind, that kind of thing only happened at night, but I guess that monsters lurk at all hour of the day.

Five minutes later I was standing in front of the gym. I hoped that I could get a membership this late in the evening. I walked in the door and went to the counter.

"What can I do for you, Miss?" the woman at the counter asked.

"I'd like to get a gym membership."

"Okay. Here are our plans," she said holding out a paper with various memberships described.

"I need the cheapest one that lets me use the pool whenever I want to."

She nodded and handed me a sheet of paper to fill out. All the normal information. Name, address, the liability waiver. I filled everything out and handed it back to her along with the debit card with my name on it.

It only took a few minutes, and she handed me the debit card and my new membership card.

"Do you have any swimsuits for sale?" I asked.

She nodded. "There's a store right over there," pointing around the corner.

The store was filled with all sorts of health and fitness supplies. Supplements, tennis rackets, gloves, and swimsuits. I picked a one-piece out and bought it.

Walking down the hall, I saw that there was no one else in the pool right then. I went to the locker room and changed into the swimsuit before heading to the pool.

Suddenly, Mexico flashed through my mind. Walking out of the back door, I retraced the steps in my mind and in the gym at the same time. I stepped down the stairs and walked to a center lane.

No goggles. No stretching. No warm-up. Just swim.

And the water remembered me. Or did I remember the water? It didn't matter. Here or Mexico, it didn't matter. Everything was the same again. Freedom. Floating. One kick after the other. One stroke after the other.

Thirty-two laps didn't feel like it had before. My muscles were used to thirty-two, and they barely burned by the end of it. I just kept going. Stroke after stroke without stopping.

I got to forty and almost stopped. My lungs burned. My legs ached. My shoulders were exhausted. "One more," I told myself.

Stroke after stroke, I crossed the pool a final time. It was like time slowed down again. Like I was riding Eeyore and I didn't have to think about going forward. I just did.

And my mind was free. Why had I pushed myself away from Angel? Because his life was full of darkness and madness? Yet, we had spent a month together and that month held every single happy memory of my life.

He had pushed me away because he didn't want me to have to live a life with pain and sadness, but pain and sadness was everywhere. The men who walked the streets who had never known anything as bad as my life still felt pain and sadness. Most of them had less happiness in their eyes than I did. I had felt pain and sadness before meeting Angel. I'd even had it before meeting Marcos.

There is no life without pain and sadness. The difference was that Angel brought me happiness. He would die eventually. Either in a blaze of gunfire or in prison. Until then, he'd bring me the happiness that every human on the planet longed for.

How could I turn away from even another week of a life with him? I didn't need him now. I could survive on my own. I could hold a job and cook my own food and take care of myself.

There was more to life than surviving though. I'd survived in a cell, but I didn't want that. I wanted the bliss that I'd felt in Mexico. I wanted to feel the freedom to scream, to writhe in his arms as he punished me with pleasure.

I didn't want to survive. I wanted to live.

My hand touched the wall, and I stood up. I was not a child to be told what to do. I was a woman. A human. And I was alive again.

And I was going to have the man that I loved.

Chapter 26: Hearts

If there is anything that a woman should know, it is love. She should know it, see it, feel it, and then lose it. Without that loss, without that debilitating pain she will never know how strong her love truly is.

I stepped through the apartment door with wet and unbrushed hair in the same red and black dress I'd left in. The swimsuit I'd worn was soaking through one of the sleeves as it hung over that arm.

Angel sat on my couch with the television on. He gave me one look and raised an eyebrow. "Found something better than dinner, I guess?"

I grinned at him. "I needed to swim, and I needed to think. Is everything cleaned up?" I asked, seriousness weaving its way into my voice.

He nodded. "Everything's taken care of."

"Then I think we need to talk." He raised his eyebrow again and sat up a little straighter.

"What about?"

"Angel, I'm not a normal girl."

"I know that. You're beautiful and funny and smart and a bunch of other things."

"No, that's not what I mean. I've seen too many things. Done too many things. I can't be this normal girl surviving in a little one-bedroom apartment. I can't date a cute guy from work and have some normal soft and cuddly sex with him once a week. I can't be that girl."

"I killed a man tonight. I shoved my thumbs into his eyeballs until they popped. Then I stabbed him through the neck and watched him bleed. And I smiled. I still smile when I think about him lying there making that gurgling sound."

Angel started to say something, and I stopped him. "No. I've listened to you every step of the way since you stole me away from Marcos. I've done it all your way. Every bit of it. I swam when I was supposed to swim. I rode when you said it was okay. I ate your food and I fucked how you wanted to fuck. Now, it's time for you to listen to me."

He stopped and he listened, his eyes perking up. "I'm not a normal girl, and I'll never be a normal girl. That's okay. I don't want to be one. But I don't want to be me without you. I've survived my entire life, but it was only when I was with you that I was happy."

"I want to be happy, Angel. Unequivocally and unapologetically happy. That isn't going to happen with another man. It doesn't have anything to do with the things you do. It's not your cooking or your money or the way you use that fantastic cock of yours."

He smirked at that last comment, but he stayed silent. "It's the way that you understand me. You had complete control of me for three weeks, and every moment of it was ecstasy. You pushed me to be stronger. You put my pieces back together. You built me when I thought that I could never be human again."

"More than anything though, you lit a fire inside of me. You gave me life, not a life, but that thing that so many people walking these streets lack. You breathed the desire for happiness into a body that had known nothing but pain."

"You took me out of my cage, but then you brought me here. To this world of nothingness, of normalcy, a cage with invisible walls. I might have been happy here. At least I didn't have the pain here. Except that now I know what freedom is. It's the ecstasy I felt with you in Mexico. I felt like I was flying the entire time, but now you've clipped my wings and thrown me into the cage again."

"You do terrible things, but so does everyone else. The evil of the world lies in every heart. Even mine. I don't care about it. I don't care about the other people. I would sacrifice every last one of them for the life that I felt on that farmhouse."

I paused for a moment and looked at him. Surprise was written all over his face. "I want to call you Master again. If you'll have me."

That was all I had. Every emotion that had swelled inside of me for the past week had ripped through me in my speech. Anger, frustration, longing, and desperation had woven themselves into my plea.

"Of course I'll have you, Maia. I only pushed you away because I wanted you to be free of me and the life I live. I'm not the good guy, Maia. You know that."

I shook my head. "There aren't any good guys, Angel. You're my good guy. You saved me when you didn't have to. You built me when you didn't have to. Even if you aren't the good guy, you make me happy, and I think that's enough."

He stood up and took me in his arms. I felt the tears begin to fall down my cheeks. I hadn't known that I needed to cry.

"I'll take you back on one condition," he said as he lifted my chin to look at him.

"Anything."

"I don't want you to call me Master. I want you to call me husband." The tears fell like a river as I smiled at him, wider than ever before.

"Of course I'll call you husband," I said.

Chapter 27: Vows

*The words mattered little. Just little
sounds to fill a waiting silence. The
promise was what mattered. The promise
that no one else mattered. Not their
friends and not their enemies. Only those
two who had bound their hearts and souls
together.*

I wore white on the day of my wedding. How anyone thought that the virginal color suited me was beyond me, but they didn't know my story, didn't know about the brand that crossed my skin.

It didn't matter. It was a beautiful dress regardless of how itchy and heavy it was. I'd seen wedding dresses that had been sleek and sexy, but they didn't feel like wedding dresses. They didn't fit the picture of Cinderella and her prince in my mind. Angel had agreed.

Although I rarely felt at home in a lot of clothes, I could appreciate the dress. I'd grown up knowing about wedding dresses, never expecting to be in one, but fantasizing about a Prince Charming who would come and save me and then we'd end up happily ever after with me in a white dress.

Maybe that was exactly what had happened? Maybe Angel was my Prince Charming, my dark knight. Whether I fit the story or not didn't matter. What mattered was that after today I was his and he was mine. Forever.

Flowers were everywhere. More than I'd ever seen in my life. Whites and blues with names I'd never heard of. And people everywhere as well.

Angel was an important man. I hadn't understood how important, but the men that had gathered had expensive suits and rode in limousines. The women had dresses that could have graced a red carpet and jewelry that would entice many thieves.

None of it mattered though. This was the expectation. We lived in his world together now, and a real marriage was a ceremony he had to go through. It kept me safe by publicly acknowledging me as his wife.

It meant that anyone who hurt me would die, and that anyone who claimed a connection to him would help to hunt the man down. You could kill a man, but you didn't touch his wife. Something about honor and innocence.

It was bullshit most likely, but that didn't change the fact that the ritual had to be done. I was going to enjoy it. It would be my only wedding, and there was nothing that would change that.

My hair was blond again, and it was growing out, nearly touching my shoulders now. I still swam every day. I'd stopped trying to increase my lap count every day at seventy-five. Instead, I swam because I loved it and because it was the one place that even now I could lose myself.

After the wedding, we were going to honeymoon in the Virgin Islands where Angel had promised that we'd spend at least one day scuba diving for fun instead of as an escape plan.

Angel had gone on six jobs since the night that I killed a man. Each time, he'd been gone for several weeks and hadn't been able to talk to me. Each time, I'd worried. Each time, he'd come back.

I knew that eventually he wouldn't. That was what I was signing up for. That was the agreement that we'd made.

I also knew that when that happened, I would never stop waiting for him. There would never be another man to replace him. I would never have another wedding.

And so I was determined to enjoy this one.

The music began to play, and I began to walk. A small Mexican girl that I didn't know threw flowers in front of me as I walked. I ignored her, hoping that she didn't trip. I had eyes for only one person in the room.

Angel's face held nothing but happiness today. He was a hard man, but not today. A wide smile crossed his face as his eyes twinkled. He held his hands behind his back and stood tall. Our eyes never left each other's as I walked down the aisle.

I stood on the other side of the altar. Though our bodies both faced the priest, we didn't stop looking at each other. Neither of us had ever expected to be married. Yet, we'd still managed to find a partner that fit us perfectly, who knew the side of us that mattered.

The priest talked about the meaning of marriage, and we ignored it. The words he said didn't matter. We knew what we were promising. We knew what marriage meant for us. There would be no divorce. We knew the evils that hid within each other. We just didn't care.

"Angel and Maia have decided to write their own vows," the priest said.

"Maia," he said, seeming surprisingly nervous.

"I fell in love with you before I knew anything about you. I couldn't admit it to anyone, not even myself, but it was there. The longer I was around you, the more I needed to know you. The more I needed to know how a girl could keep that spark of life alive even in the worst scenarios."

"And I realized that I only had one purpose during our time together. I needed to feed that spark, to give that fire inside of you a chance to live like it should have from the very beginning."

"Maia, I am only a man, and I cannot promise to keep you safe from everything. I cannot promise to live forever to keep you happy. I will do my best to be there for you in any way possible, but I can only *promise* two things. I promise that I will love you forever, and I promise that I will do anything to keep that fire inside of you burning, even if I must smother my own to do so."

He put the same white gold ring on my finger than he'd given me during our three-hour marriage, and I smiled at him. It didn't feel heavy anymore.

I took a deep breath and said loudly enough for the audience to hear,

"Angel, you are my Prince Charming, my knight in shining armor. You've saved me from the evils of the world, and you've given me a chance at a life worth living."

"That life wasn't worth living without you, my love. You will always be my knight, but I've learned that even knights get tired. Even knights need to be held. Even knights need to know that they are not alone in the world."

"I can promise you that I will wait for you. Always. The world may crumble, but at the end of the world, I'll still be waiting for you. I will always love you, and I will always be the woman you need, no matter what that may be."

I took the white gold ring that he'd worn and placed it on his finger. His was a matching ring, except that instead of fruit, small thorns covered the vines. In the center was a single diamond that had been inset in the ring, almost as though it had been hidden behind the vines. He smiled, and his eyes shimmered in the light.

"Angel and Maia, I now pronounce you husband and wife. Angel, you may kiss your bride."

He took my face his hands, and he bent down to kiss me. Lips touching like fireworks. Electricity radiated from our bodies, and I felt like I was kissing him for the first time. He was mine. Forever.

Epilogue

A sword does not become strong without heat and pressure. Only through tempering, one hammer blow and one fire at a time, does it become strong enough and sharp enough to survive the ravages of war.

She's perfect in every way," I said. "We're going on our honeymoon tomorrow."

"Congratulations are in order, then." The voice on the other end of the phone seemed happy. He should be with how much he charged, but at the end of the day, it was worth every last penny.

"Did she ever figure it out?"

"No, she's still completely sure that you're dead. You're a hell of an actor, and that warehouse was as good as a movie set."

"I've sold many girls to 'heroes'. It isn't difficult to trick a slave into anything with just a bit of experience. They want to believe it's true so badly that they only need a little push and no time to look closely."

"I don't know. It was pretty convincing to me. The gunshots especially were realistic. How'd you make the dust fly next to the truck when we escaped?"

"I used real bullets and excellent snipers."

I paused for a second taking that bit of information in. We could have been shot at any time. It didn't matter since we weren't, but I was glad that our dealings would come to a close soon enough.

"Was the branding really necessary?" I asked. It had bothered me from the very beginning.

"Of course. Everything was necessary. Without that, she'd forget what you did. She'd forget what she could have become. Now, she holds her past as a trophy, doesn't she?"

"Yes. It's infuriating how well you work, but we all have our specialties. Thank God I'm not in yours. I'd have to vomit every day. She was so young."

"It had to be that way. I promise, it is as streamlined as possible."

"How are the men that I hit with the firebomb?"

"They're fine. They knew what they were walking into and were prepared. They were paid well enough that none of them complained about the few burns that they received."

"That's good to hear. Did you know that she killed the man that you sent to rape her at her apartment?"

"I didn't send anyone. Once you left Veracruz, I simply waited. You took the prescribed seven days away from her, correct?"

"I took the seven days, but what do you mean that you didn't send anyone? A man tried to rape her, and she killed him. Popped his fucking eyeballs with her thumbs and then drove his own knife through his neck."

"That had nothing to do with me. Purely coincidence. I'd say it was a lucky thing then."

"I guess so. I'm glad that I had started teaching her self-defense."

There was a pause.

"I guess that our business is done now. I will authorize the second half of the payment when I get off the phone. I truly hope that I never have to see or talk to you again, Marcos."

"That is something we can both agree on, Angel."

CPSIA information can be obtained
at www.ICGtesting.com
Printed in the USA
LVHW020814010423
743223LV00027B/1352